Born in Melbourne, Victoria, Portia Stanton-Noble currently lives in the Gilbert Valley, South Australia with her son. When she was eight years old. she had already made up her mind that she was going to be a writer.

This novel is the third instalment of the series, following *The Big Dead Dry* and *Pretty Dead Ordinary*.

Since completing her trilogy of murder mysteries and romantic intrigues surrounding her characters in the fictional township of Brumby Flat, she has been busy researching material for her next books.

For my dear friend, Pamela Zanker, and to Elaine and Neil Lamond, with fond memories of Geelong, Victoria.

Portia Stanton-Noble

DROP DEAD LIKE FLIES

AUSTIN MACAULEY PUBLISHERS™
LONDON • CAMBRIDGE • NEW YORK • SHARJAH

Copyright © Portia Stanton-Noble 2023

The right of Portia Stanton-Noble to be identified as author of this work has been asserted by the author in accordance with sections 77 and 78 of the Copyright, Designs and Patents Act 1988.

All rights reserved. No part of this publication may be reproduced, stored in a retrieval system, or transmitted in any form or by any means, electronic, mechanical, photocopying, recording, or otherwise, without the prior permission of the publishers.

Any person who commits any unauthorised act in relation to this publication may be liable to criminal prosecution and civil claims for damages.

This is a work of fiction. Names, characters, businesses, places, events, locales, and incidents are either the products of the author's imagination or used in a fictitious manner. Any resemblance to actual persons, living or dead, or actual events is purely coincidental.

A CIP catalogue record for this title is available from the British Library.

ISBN 9781035803071 (Paperback)
ISBN 9781035803088 (ePub e-book)

www.austinmacauley.com

First Published 2023
Austin Macauley Publishers Ltd®
1 Canada Square
Canary Wharf
London
E14 5AA

I have to acknowledge the continued support of my family for my work. I am so fortunate to be living in a region of South Australia which is abundant with talented and supportive fellow writers.

Prologue

The family rolled up in their large SUV vehicle at a clearing in the Beecham's Bridge National Park. They all agreed that it was the perfect place to hold their picnic. The sun was shining bright in a clear blue sky.

The young couple from Adelaide began to unpack their picnic gear from the back of the vehicle while their two young children ran excitedly around the car, playing a game of chasey.

Their mother lost her temper after the boy, her son, had bumped into her leg a second time.

"Hey, stop it, Carl. Stop running like crazy."

"Sorry, mummy. Can we please look around a bit?"

She turned to look at her husband who nodded and said in a low voice, "Yeah. Let them run off some steam."

He then turned on his heel and said sternly, shaking his forefinger at them, "Okay now, kids. Don't you wander off too far. Make sure that you can still see us."

"Yes, daddy," Carl nodded his agreement, but his sister Britney just stood there, holding her favourite bunny rabbit in a headlock. She was two years younger than Carl but had already developed a formidable, stubborn personality.

"Come on, sis," Carl reached out and grabbed Britney's small pale hand into his own.

They ran off together, into the trees. After a moment, Carl looked behind them.

"I can't see them," he exclaimed.

"Where are they?"

"Oh. It's okay. If I stand on my tippy-toes, I can see them."

"Oh good," Britney shook her head and threw her bunny around, "I don't want to get lost."

Carl smiled, "We won't get lost."

"Can we play hide and seek? Please?"

"Yeah okay. I'll go hide. You count to five. Then you count to five again."

He knew his little sister could only count up to the number five. She put her hands over her eyes after she had put her toy bunny carefully down on the dirt floor.

Carl also knew that he couldn't go far away, so he found a bush next to him and crawled under it. He had to push himself forward using his elbows and knees. He looked down and realised the front of his t-shirt was smeared by dirt, but he had gone so far that he wasn't prepared to go back now. He knew his mother would be cross with him for getting himself and his clothes so grubby. Suddenly, the low-lying bush disappeared, and he carefully got up and brushed the dirt off the knees of his elastic waist jeans.

"Oh wow," he gasped, his brown eyes wide. He had stumbled onto a burnt-out vehicle. It was in bad shape, but it was still obvious what it was. He walked closer up to it and put his hands on the burnt window frame.

He turned his head when he heard leaves rustling and he saw it was Britney. She emerged from the bushes, dragging her toy bunny after her.

"Carl, you made it too easy for me. I saw you go in," she said crossly, in her small voice.

"Look at this, Brit," he cried, "I found us a bus."

She frowned and remarked, "It looks like a truck."

"I'm going to drive the bus," he said excitedly, lunging ahead to claim the driver's seat which was just a frame and a small square of upholstery.

"Why are you driving it?"

"Because you're too little," he grabbed the steering wheel which turned in his hands a couple of times before completely falling off. He then pretended that he was holding a steering wheel.

Britney climbed onto the steel frame on the passenger side but found she had nothing to sit on. She stood up, holding onto what was left of the dashboard and holding her bunny up by its ears.

"Vrooooommm, varoom…" Carl proceeded to make a barrage of various car noises while his sister looked on. She directed him through imaginary roads full of traffic.

Their fun came to an abrupt end when their father's concerned voice finally reached them.

"We're here, daddy. Look. We found a bus," Britney yelled out.

A couple of minutes passed until they saw him crawl out from the bushes. He straightened up and glared at them playing in the burnt-out vehicle.

"What are you two doing? Get away from that old car. It's dangerous."

He walked forward and his foot hit something hard, like metal in the ground. He stopped. Something had told him to look down. He dropped to his knees and scattered the dirt and leaf debris away from the hard square shaped object.

"What is it, daddy?" Britney had appeared next to him, looking at the same spot too.

"I don't know, sweetie," he grabbed his pocket knife out of his jeans side pocket and started to dig around the metal object. It took a few minutes and a bit of an effort to remove the small rusty metal box out of the ground.

"I think this has been here for a very long time," he said. He pried it open with brute strength and found some old, faded photographs and some old one-dollar notes folded over inside.

"Is it buried treasure?" Carl asked, grinning like any six-year-old would who loves reading adventure books.

"Daddy, I found this too," Britney held up a bullet between her fingers.

"Put it down," her father snapped at her.

She immediately dropped the bullet on the ground. Tears started to well up in her eyes and she held her cuddly toy tight against her chest. Her father put down the metal box. He held out both his arms, and softly embraced her.

"I'm sorry, sweetie. I didn't mean to yell at you. It's just that…I think we have to tell mummy what you've found. And we'll have to call the police too. We'll talk about it later, okay?"

Clutching the box under his right arm and holding Britney's small hand in his other, he led his children quietly away. He was certain that they had inadvertently stumbled across a crime scene.

Chapter One

Raquel Willaston brushed stray strands of her blonde hair out of her hazel eyes with her wrist. She flicked the switch on the electric kettle by her elbow. She was elbow deep in flour, in the middle of making a base for her lemon cheesecake. She was now preparing an oven tray in Bette and Phil Duncan's large blackwood kitchen. She knew her failings as a cook but if she put her mind to it, she was very good at baking cakes and pastries. Soon after the tragic murder of her best friend Bette, she had moved into Bette's sprawling three-storey home in Brumby Flat. She was now sharing the bed of her friend's widowed husband Senior Detective Phillip Duncan.

Quite naturally, locals in the small town were standing around in their street clusters, whispering and speculating on their rapid-fire coupling. It was a first-class scandal unfolding under their watchful eyes. Raquel hated gossip and kept her distance from the rumour mongers as far as she could. Whenever she worked at the Raindrops Shop, locals came in for coffee but glared at her loudly and she heard their silence. She was okay with that.

For the last two weeks, she had hardly seen much of Duncan. He was staying fifty kilometres away, in a motel room at Beecham's Bridge National Park. A new crime scene had unfolded up there which demanded his attention, with the discovery of two bodies long buried in shallow graves within the perimeters of the park. A burnt-out kombi van had been found nearby and there was reasonable evidence to suggest the bodies were of his hippie parents who had disappeared over thirty years ago.

Suddenly, Raquel's cake preparations were interrupted when she heard a loud, persistent knocking at the kitchen back door. She turned around and wiped her flour dusted hands on the apron she was wearing over her favourite floral dress and secretly wondered if Duncan had returned. Perhaps, he had accidentally misplaced his house keys, she thought to herself. He had left the house over an hour ago, saying he had to drop by the local police station and then return to the park.

She quickly realised how wrong she was as soon as she unlatched the screen door. She came face to face with an attractive younger woman with auburn dyed, shoulder length hair, dressed in a figure-hugging leopard print wrap dress. Her eyes were a large pale blue-green and when she smiled, her lips were wide and shiny with cherry coloured lip gloss. They had met previously in the Raindrops Shop, but Raquel was too rattled to remember their meeting.

She smiled briefly at the strange woman and took a sharp intake of air into her lungs.

"Hello, I'm Geena Henderson," the strange woman announced, smiling and then automatically thrust her pale freckled hand out.

Raquel very reluctantly shook her outstretched hand. She could feel the hair on the back of her neck bristling.

"Hello. How can I help you?"

Geena smiled again, her bright red shiny lips pulled tight.

"I am looking for Phil Duncan."

"He's not here, at the moment. But can I help you?"

Geena brushed past her, teetering on her matching leopard print stilettos and flicked her confident eyes around the kitchen, like she knew the place well. She certainly knew to use the back door well enough, Raquel thought to herself.

"Well, to be perfectly honest, I heard that his wife has passed away. Poor thing."

"Yes, it was very tragic. Very sudden. You read about it in the papers, I imagine. Are you a reporter? Are you family?"

"Oh no. I was just passing by, and I thought that poor Phil might want some company. A good shoulder to cry on. So, here I am. Just passing through town, on my way far north."

Raquel bit down on her bottom lip and said, "I'm sorry but what do you mean *exactly*?"

Geena made a tittering noise deep in her throat, "You must know…what I mean. We're both mature women, after all."

"I'm sorry, Geena, I have no idea what you are on about."

"Well. The poor man has needs. I know Phil. I'd just like to catch up with him."

"Well. Right then," Raquel put her flour dusted hands on her hips and said in a clear, no-nonsense tone of voice, "I guess I'll have to spell it out. I *am* his company. We are together."

"Oh, I see," Geena suddenly looked uncomfortable.

"But sure thing, Geena. I will pass on your most heartfelt sympathy to my Phil. I attended my best friends' funeral, his wife. I believed in him when everyone else around here thought he was a killer. Still, it's very nice of you to show up, out of the blue. Uninvited. But I think you should go now. I'll mention to him you were just passing through, expressing your utmost concern for him."

Geena folded her arms and stood her ground for a long moment, staring into her taller rival's wide hazel eyes. Finally, she relaxed her gaze, cast her eyes to the floor and turned to leave.

"You know, he may just call me up one day. I think he's still got my number."

Raquel shrugged her shoulders, her hazel eyes narrowed to slits and helpfully, she even opened the screen door wide for the younger woman.

"Well. You keep hoping for that. I sincerely doubt that he will. You're not really his type."

She slammed the screen door soundly behind Geena who looked on with her pretty mouth wide open. Then she finalised their brief encounter by closing the back door firmly in her face.

Unfortunately, Raquel knew perfectly well that Geena Henderson was in fact his type. She clenched her right fist and realised she would have to ask Duncan how he knew this woman, but somehow, she had an idea already. She blinked away a tear as she saw an image of Bette's face. She remembered that Bette had raised the suspicion that Duncan had cheated on her early into their marriage. The recent encounter with Geena left no doubt in her mind that Duncan had strayed briefly.

She returned her attention to her cake making and decided to forget about the encounter with Geena.

****

Every morning all year round, she was awake by five o'clock. It was no different that day too. If it was a particularly quiet night, she would manage to get a good, solid six hours of sleep but she wasn't the type to complain. She knew she had a good roof over her head, and she was making more money than she knew what to do with. She stretched her limbs and yawned with abundance. She looked down and realised that she had slept in her working clothes again. She rolled out of bed and prepared herself for the brisk six am start.

Banksia Ava Peterson was busy running the family's roadhouse single-handedly, very much on her own. The Batty Roadhouse stood on the very edge of Beecham's Bridge National Park, overshadowed by surrounding large, towering gumtrees. Not to mention the thick blanket of fog which tended to shroud it in secrecy during the winter months. The long-haul truckies always knew it was there.

After a brief freshen up in the bathroom, she took up her usual position behind the shop counter, wiping away the dust, which she challenged to a battle every single day. After a short, furious attempt at cleaning it, she fumbled with the bunch of keys in her hand, found the front door key and switched on the sliding doors of the shop.

She had a square face with a pointed chin. Her forehead was too high, and her soft brown eyes were deep set. She had a generous but curvy figure and looked outwardly plain, as she often wore her light brown over the shoulder length hair in a high, unflattering, tight bun. There was a thin layer of foundation on her plump face and to finish her makeup, she added just a little tease of mascara to her eyelashes. Her hair was usually curly, so the severe bun controlled its tendency to frizz up, particularly as the long work day rolled on.

Due to the nature of her daily work, she almost always wore a simple black t-shirt teamed with a pair of stretch jeans. All day, she was pretty much on her feet. There was a lot to do around the Batty Roadhouse. Fortunately for her, it was a business which was sporadically busy. It was situated on the side of a main highway, but there was a small town only fifty kilometres away, so most road traffic just drove straight past.

Those who did stop at the Batty were mainly the long-haul truck drivers, dropping by for takeaway food or fuel and curious tourists who came to visit the big fruit bat statue or the national park. However, more often than not, it was the local farmers who dropped in for either a coffee, a hot meal, a cold beer or a good yak. The licensed bar at the roadhouse often stayed open until ten o'clock at night or when the last patron finally left the premises. Banksia was also in charge of the weighbridge there, and for cleaning and managing the three-unit motel at the rear of the roadhouse building. She collected all the eggs each morning from the chicken coop too. She was also responsible for sorting the local's mail. The locals came into the roadhouse at least once a week, to collect all their letters and parcels. She also carried some envelopes, stamps and basic parcel packs for them.

The separate motel units at the rear were often empty, but this week had been unusually different. A city detective had rocked up, flashed his impressive credentials at her and moved in. He largely kept to himself and walked the back trails during the days. She knew that he went on long jogs early in the morning.

She knew why he was hanging around. In fact, it was the talk of all the locals. A burnt-out old kombi van had been found covered in thick underbrush in the national park several weeks ago. A couple of children had accidentally discovered the vehicle. Teams of police officers had arrived, scanning the surrounding bushland for clues and evidence. They traversed that section of the park for a good three weeks. Two badly decomposed bodies were unearthed nearby.

Banksia wasn't at all that shocked by the discovery of the bodies buried in shallow graves within the park. There had been whispers for the last two decades that strange, unsavoury characters were forever wandering in and out of Beecham's Bridge National Park. In fact, she was certain she sometimes entertained these people in her bar and served them meals in the roadhouse dining room. But she knew how to handle the undesirables who came through the door. She had several surveillance cameras installed in the shop and bar, hooked up to be viewed by her parents in the rear cottage where they lived. Banksia was not too sure if her parents actually viewed the footage daily, but for all intents and purposes, the cameras were rolling twenty-four hours a day. She also knew when and how to raise her voice whenever it was needed. As soon as she let out her best growl and slammed her fist on the bar counter, the bad behaviour ceased.

Her parents Janine and Bob Peterson were no longer seen out in public these days. They had abandoned the running of the Batty Roadhouse to their daughter over six years ago. They lived in the old stone cottage well behind the roadhouse while Banksia lived in the large backroom off to the left of the industrial kitchen. The roadhouse was originally owned and run by Banksia's Great Aunty Mabel.

Mabel had come out from Ireland when in her mid-twenties and forged her own new life in Australia. She left her family behind and none of them understood her need to migrate. She had landed in Sydney at a time when life was fairly simple and uncomplicated. She was fortunate enough to walk straight into a retail job in a large department store. Like all the ladies at that time, she was never seen outside without her straw hat with a spray of flowers on it and wearing a pair of white lace gloves.

After three years of full-time work at the department store, Mabel made the snap decision to go on a road trip to South Australia. She boarded an interstate bus and only got off when she saw the roadhouse gleaming like an unpolished jewel within the shadows of Beecham's Bridge National Park. The bus driver was not keen to pull to a stop in the middle of nowhere, but Mabel was insistent, shouting at him to stop and rattling the bus door with her gloved right hand. The tyres had squealed to a halt roughly twenty metres down the road. As soon as her medium heeled court shoes landed on the gravel and dirt road verge, it felt like she was finally home. In one hand, she held her suitcase and in the other, she held her black vinyl handbag high on her wrist.

Mabel walked confidently into the roadhouse and found the owner incoherently drunk and sprawled over the well-worn pool table. He had a big barrel of a chest and very tall, and although she was slight in build, she managed to half drag him to a nearby table. She pushed him onto an old chair and propped his head up on the tabletop edge. She spent the rest of the afternoon medicating him with multiple cups of hot lemon and myrtle tea until he could form his words and make a proper sentence.

The owner was a local farmer called Jack who wanted to spend more time with his prize-winning merino sheep, rather than being tied to running the roadhouse. As it happened,

Mabel had saved half the money required to buy the business from him, in fact local legend had it that she had tipped her black vinyl handbag upside down and put it all on the table in front of him, right under his nose.

"There. That's all the money I've got in the world."

He had removed his dusty old hat, squinted his eyes and had said to her, "Righto. How about this then? Double or nothing in a card game, Missus? A game of poker?"

She had nodded her head. She had never played Poker before, and she had told him so. Jack was fairly sure he had a good chance of keeping his business and taking all of her precious life savings as well. He also added another element of surprise, by stipulating it would have to be a game of strip Poker. Mabel was a bit of a prude, but she had her heart and mind firmly set on owning and running the roadhouse at any cost. She agreed to his absurd and altogether rather unpleasant proposal. They sealed the deal with a solid handshake between them.

Two hours later, they had arrived at the crucial point of playing the last hand. Mabel was seated calmly at the kitchen table, still wearing her dress, straw hat, gloves, and only minus her handknitted cardigan. However, poor old farmer Jack was right down to his boxer shorts and moth eaten, discoloured singlet.

"Okay, lady. Show us what you got," he grinned, as he put down four of a kind face up on the table. He looked on as proud as a peacock. He grinned broadly, certain he had won the day with his last hand.

Mabel shook her head and made a face of defeat, but miraculously she turned over a royal flush.

"I guess it means I've won, Jack? I've won the lot?" She chirped.

Jack had slumped down in his chair. He had lost his singlet and his business too that fateful evening, but he still had his paddocks of sheep, his dignity and his old farmhouse. Jack had picked up his discarded clothes, boots and quietly retreated into the cool of the evening.

With Jack gone, she finally had the time to survey the roadhouse. She noted that the business had obviously started to suffer from his neglect. Fortunately, Mabel removed her hat and gloves right there and then. She just popped on her apron which she had neatly packed in her luggage and immediately took charge of the unruly mess.

Over the years, Mabel managed to save the takings money and had the impressive upside-down fibreglass fruit bat statue specially built as a tourist attraction. She had been told that native bats were in abundance in the park, and she knew how much Australians loved big attractions. The original plan for the standing bat statue had a wingspan of nine metres. It proved to be too big, and she realised it would stand too close to the fuel pumps. It was also going to cost more than her modest budget would allow. In the end, the standing bat was replaced with an upside-down bat, its wings clasped against its sides for reasons of economics.

Once the statue was installed, she officially changed the business name to the Batty Roadhouse. Outsiders referred to it as the 'Big Bat' and for the next three decades, it was a tourist attraction. But once the nations obsession with 'big' things cooled, the bat statue started to fall into a sad state of disrepair. Mabel just let it happen. She continued to sell postcards of the 'Big Bat' in its glory days to interested tourists.

Much later on, she had the three motel rooms built at the back of the roadhouse. She also had an extra diesel pump installed for the trucks. The takeaway proved popular with locals and the long-haul truckies driving through. The roadhouse kitchen went through a number of upgrades.

She never had a husband or children and lived like a recluse from the rest of the family. She lived only to work the roadhouse, so it came as a complete surprise when she suddenly carked it and her Will stated she had left everything she owned to the Petersons. They had never met her and in the Will package, they only inherited two photographs of Mabel. One was a faded black and white picture of a headstrong young woman, clutching an oversize suitcase at a ship dock. It was taken on the day she landed in Sydney, Australia. Banksia was struck by this early image of her great aunty. She had light coloured short hair, with wild big curls. Her eyes were large, her nose a little too big and a generous mouth. She was painfully slim, dressed in a plain cardigan over a peter pan collar dress.

The other photograph was in colour of her as an old woman, hunched over, her features vastly changed by age lines and snow-white hair pulled back in a tight bun. She was seen pouring a beer for a beaming, red faced truck driver. The locals often entertained Banksia with some of their amazing stories and fond recollections of her great aunty Mabel. She was something of an urban legend around the district.

However, Janine and Bob Peterson proved to be completely hopeless at running The Batty. For a start, they lacked Mabel's drive and passion for making a dollar. Janine had accidentally set fire to the kitchen one night and the takeaway was abandoned for three months. That was the moment when the business really started to go backwards, and they quickly thrust their daughter Banksia into the foreground. They now spent most of their days sitting in their well-worn armchairs watching pay television channels or surfing the internet. They were gifted, clever people, both had university degrees. Her father Bob had been a professor in Trigonometry. They were so clever in fact, that they left their only child in charge of their new business, and she proved to them she was more than capable. They happily retreated from public life, eating junk food and consuming sugary drinks. They only communicated with Banksia through the intercom in the kitchen. Mostly, they were asking her to bring them a serve of fish and chips or more soft drink cans. She would have to leave it outside their latched kitchen door. Sometimes, they even asked how she was feeling. She always put on her best, sweet voice and answered that she was fine. She only told them what she believed they wanted to hear.

But every day, Banksia Peterson was thinking very seriously about her escape. She had nothing concrete planned as yet, but she had the roadhouse so well organised, she believed any fool could walk right in and manage it. When the petrol pump needed to be used, a honking sound would emit from the till. The sliding front door opening would start a tingle of bells. If the weight bridge was needed, a beeping sensor would go off. If someone rang the bell at the motel units, it chimed away on the intercom. If someone entered the bar area, it would trigger a row of cow bells. She was also the local fruit fly inspector, so sometimes she did a random roadside blitz.

After thoroughly dusting the counter tops, Banksia busied herself with wiping the wine glasses clean, to prepare for bar work later on. There was nothing she couldn't do at the Batty Roadhouse.

An hour passed by when Senior Detective Phillip Duncan was seen walking towards the sliding doors of the roadhouse. Banksia had a guess that he must be at least forty. Too old to hold her attention for long but she had admired him secretly under her dark eyelashes since he had arrived. He was at least tall, he had a trim well-proportioned build, a strong chest and the glasses he wore made him look distinguished and intelligent. He had a strong, deep voice which commanded attention.

She noticed he was conservatively attired in plain white shirt, aqua toned tie and plain tan trousers. He had very little hair, which was trimmed short to his scalp, but it suited him well. In the morning, she had seen him go off on his daily jog through the park. He would be gone for more than an hour.

Duncan was trying hard to not to show his emotions to the people around him. It had been a tough fortnight for him. He was still waiting for forensics to formally identify the remains of the bodies found buried in a swallow grave near the kombi van. So far, all that was certain was the gender of the bodies, confirmed to be that of a man and a woman in their early twenties. He spent quite some time at the burial site when he arrived, trying to prepare himself for the worst possible scenario. As much as he wanted closure about what had happened to his hippie parents over thirty years ago, another part of him dreaded learning the truth.

He often recalled the last time he saw them. He was just seven years old at the time when his parents dropped him off at his grandparents' home in Surfers Paradise. He remembered that they had both bent down, kissed his soft chubby cheeks and enthusiastically waved him goodbye as they drove off, on their way to join a hitchhiking tour of Tibet. If they were, in fact, killed within the perimeters of Beecham's Bridge National Park, they were hundreds of kilometres off their course. It would add more questions, rather than answers for Phil Duncan to unravel.

On top of that, he was also dealing with his murdered wife's funeral which had finally happened a week ago. If not for Raquel's hand slipped into his own and her words of support in his ear, he didn't know how he would have made it through that terrible day. It was hard to get up to the podium at the local funeral home and present the eulogy to half the town who turned up, who had either attended their wedding or the reception just months before. His hands were shaking right through it, but Raquel's hand was warm, firm in his and she proved to be a reassuring presence. He had truly loved his wife Bette, but Raquel was a tangible link to this recent past. Through her, he still felt connected to his Bette.

As he entered the roadhouse sliding doors, he gave Banksia a slight, tight-lipped smile and nodded politely when he saw her. His bright blue eyes sparkled momentarily behind his glasses. But it was brief and then his serious expression returned.

"Well, Detective Duncan, are you enjoying your accommodation and our hospitality?" She asked him cheerily, wiping another wine glass clean.

He shrugged his broad shoulders, "Call me Phil. Yeah. It's okay. I'm not staying long. I'm just here for another day or so. I came looking for some breakfast," he sunk down onto a bar stool in front of her. It dropped two inches as soon as he applied his weight to it. Banksia made a mental note to herself to remember to fix the stool later.

"Sure thing. I can make you a full breakfast with sausages, bacon and scrambled eggs or how about a ham and cheese toastie? Your choice."

He readjusted his slipping eyeglasses on the bridge of his nose and leaned against the counter, "The toastie will do me. Enjoy working here, Miss…I'm sorry, I've forgotten your name."

"That's okay. You can call me Banksia. Or Banks. Everyone around here does. Yeah, I do. Never boring around here, believe me. You'd be surprised at all the gossip and crazy stuff that people tell me. Would even make you blush like a beetroot, detective. Phil. Still, it makes roadhouse life interesting I suppose."

"Are you the only one working here?"

She smiled, her ruddy plump cheeks rising up, "No, my parents are around too. But they are indisposed. They're very private people, my parents."

He nodded, considering her words before he continued, tactfully changing the subject.

"It's a big place. Do you get a lot of people stopping over?"

She finished twirling around the last clean wine glass and tucked a stray strand of flyaway hair over her left ear.

"Sometimes, holiday makers stop, but mainly, we get the locals in, and truckies too, filling up. Buying food, soft drinks for the road. You're a bit of rare fish out here, detective."

He smirked. He made a smacking sound with his teeth, a nervous tic that had reappeared since his wife's funeral.

"This is not where I want to be either, Banks. I am here to seek answers to the questions I have. It was shocking to find these bodies in the national park. I imagine it's been shocking for you, and the locals here too."

"Yeah. About that. I am really *not* that shocked by the discovery. There're some interesting characters who like to hang around here. I see them go into the park now and again. But I don't know if every one of them comes out, you know," she drew out the last few words and had Duncan completely mesmerised by them.

"Interesting analogy. What precisely makes you say that?"

She shrugged her shoulders, "I'm not watching the park activities twenty-four seven. I don't have the time, but usually, people drop in here before going into the park. Most come back here after too, for a drink, meal or for petrol. Then they drive off, home maybe or to their destination. From time to time, you know how you hear about people disappearing in the news? Just in general, I mean. You kind of wonder what happens to them. I think…it's easy to be hard to find in there. Inside the park. Anyway, it's just an observation. Not stating a fact, or anything. I am sure there are secrets hiding in the park. In the city, they call stuff like those urban legends, right? This is more like a rural legend."

She paused for a moment, drew a breath and then continued, "But there's also another exit from the park too.

Some may use that, rather than backing up and turning around. So, who really knows? I guess people disappear all the time."

"Where's the exit road?"

Banksia patted her hand under the front counter until she pulled out a well-worn, crumpled brochure of the park. She unfolded it, stretched out the folds and pointed to a position on the map.

"It's right here, see? Takes you onto the back roads, it's all dirt track, mind you. But really easy for a four-wheel vehicle to get through. It's about ten kilometres into the park."

Duncan craned his neck over the map and nodded understanding, "Oh wow. The park's about ten kilometres end to end? That's massive."

"About that. It might even be bigger. Not too sure. But that's the dirt track right there."

She tapped her finger again on the map.

Duncan leaned back from the counter, and the stool he was seated on spiralled down another good inch, "Well. I must go for a drive. In a better vehicle."

"Ask the park ranger, he'll help you. He's very new but he's a real nature lover."

Under the crumpled brochure, he noticed another one slip onto the floor.

He bent down and scooped it up.

"Oh wow. What's this? A folk festival?"

Her eyes widened and she nodded her head enthusiastically, "Very exciting. It's the thirty-second and a third anniversary of the original Folk Music Festival held in the park. They somehow missed the big date two years ago.

You can guess by the title, they kind of missed it again. But, hey, it will be great for the Batty. It will bring them in droves."

Suddenly, a persistent beeping noise could be heard coming from the direction of the kitchen. It startled the pair of them.

Banksia turned her head and said, "That's my parents calling me now. Back soon. Breakfast is on the way in a minute."

Duncan watched her quickly walk away and answer the intercom on the kitchen wall. Eventually, all he could hear was the muffled sounds of voices from the kitchen, but they were not very clear. He waited patiently for his breakfast to be made.

While he did, he glanced outside. He saw a flashy looking car pulled up at the front petrol pump outside, apple green in colour. A middle-aged man in a sharp navy suit and tie stepped out. On closer inspection, Duncan noted that the man actually looked closer to retirement age, with deep lines etched down his hollowed cheeks. The eyes were hooded, deep brown in colour and he had a no-nonsense air about him. He was not as tall as Duncan, thin but with a pronounced pot belly which protruded over his low-slung trousers. He looked like he'd been around the block and then some.

Duncan was right about the no-nonsense approach observation. Senior Detective Richard Bottrell certainly exuded it, and he was just five months away from retirement. For the last five years, that was all he was talking about. In fact, the entire department was sick of hearing about his big retirement plans. He lamented about spending his future days reading the daily newspaper on his porch, going fishing, cruising down the Murray River and travelling around

Australia in his caravan. He had just purchased a small tinnie for the fishing part. He was hoping this case would be his last. He had lost the passion for his job a long time ago. He had also lost his wife to another man a good decade back and his grownup children did all that they could to avoid seeing him, making up elaborate excuses.

He strode confidently through the sliding front doors of the roadhouse and nodded in Duncan's direction.

"Detective Phil Duncan? Hey, mate. I'm the new guy. I'm Rich. It's Richard but no one ever calls me that," he thrust out his tawny hand.

Duncan spun around in the stool and hesitated, before he shook his hand firmly back.

"I can see that. Nice car. I'm sorry, but who are you again?"

Rich cleared his throat, "I'm your new partner. Detective Longmeil is taking extended leave. It was very sudden, I know. Didn't they send you the message?"

"No, but I guess I'm not that surprised. I live further out these days."

"Anyway, I'm Detective Richard Bottrell. But Rich for short is fine. Have you checked your emails this morning?"

Duncan arched an eyebrow over his glasses and glanced down at his mobile phone screen, "No, not yet," he said, "I'm waiting patiently for my breakfast. It's sort of coming, I think."

"Yeah, mate, well, the forensics report is there for you, and the bodies in the park have been formerly identified. You might want to look it over, when you have a free moment."

"Am I going to be…"

Rich cut him off, "Shocked? Yeah, you may need to brace yourself, buddy. That's why I was sent here today."

Duncan shifted his weight uncomfortably on the faulty stool and stiffen his back. He was fairly sure he already knew the answers, without hearing what his new partner had to say. He knew without skimming through a departmental email what the truth actually was. He sat there, elbows on the counter. His face was ashen, and the long fingers of his hands clutched together in a steeple position.

"It's okay. I'll wait for my breakfast first."

His new partner rolled his shoulders and reached into his breast pocket, "Righto. Time for a smoke then," he remarked, removing a partially squashed packet of cigarettes.

He saw Banksia visibly frown behind the counter and he quickly added with a sly wink of an eye, "I know, lovey, it's a disgusting habit."

Chapter Two

The clearing was small, but it was a large enough stage for what was about to transpire. It was clearly the middle of the day, with bright shards of sunlight piercing through the high canopies of gum trees and shining in patches across the earth which was abundantly covered in bark pieces and leaf debris.

Lying on this brittle, dry ground cover, Shane had his right cheek pressed against it. His hands were bound, pulled tight behind his back with tow rope and his feet and knees were tied as well. Effectively, he could not move a muscle. His mouth was not gagged but he had difficulty talking anyway. He had been knocked unconscious to the ground and was finally coming around, with a mouthful of dirt and brittle gum leaves to spit out. His shoulder length light brown hair was unruly and covered in dry ground cover as well. He rolled his blue eyes open and tried to look around as far as he could turn his still throbbing head.

His yellow t-shirt clung to his back from sweat and his flared blue jeans were dirty around the knees and ankle cuffs. He was bare foot, with prickles dug firmly into his fleshy soles. His feet were hurting, but his head was pounding far worse. There was a dried trickle of blood down the left side of his face, starting from his hairline, tracing down his forehead.

Shane lifted his chin with some difficulty and scanned his surroundings again. He strained against the ropes bond around his wrists. The struggle was useless, however. He let out a groan and spit out the dirt embedded in his throat. He coughed drily and cried out, "Hello? Help, help me."

He listened for a long, anxious minute, but no answer came. He could only hear birdsong and the sound of a kookaburra cackling away somewhere nearby.

He cried out again and anxiously waited. His mind was racing with thoughts of how to escape, but the ropes were holding him firmly down.

Finally, a series of new sounds reached his ears. He heard what sounded like approaching footsteps crunching against the ground cover and a swishing sound, like an object was being dragged across the hard earth.

The object came into view, pulled up right next to him. A gloved hand dumped the frightened and gagged face of his girlfriend near him, in his vision. She looked to be in much the same shape as he was. Their assailant had dragged her along on her bare belly next to him and turned her sharply onto her right side.

"Where did you stash the money?" A voice growled next to Shane's ears.

Shane said nothing. He lay as still as he could, but his body was visibly shaking.

His Daisy lay there, her chest heaving, small branches and twigs had torn little holes and tears in her cropped t-shirt. Some twigs had penetrated her lightly tanned flesh, embedded into her breasts and she had small blotches of blood soaked into her clothes. Her bare midriff was covered in dirt and more blood. Her denim shorts were still zipped but pulled down around to her lower hips, showing the start of her pelvic bone. Her legs were also bound tightly. Shane couldn't see her arms, except her shoulders, so he assumed they were securely tied behind her back as well. Her bright blue eyes were large and expressive, pleading for his help, which he was helpless to give anyway. He couldn't move any of his hands to be of use.

Their attacker roughly removed the gag around her bleeding mouth, and she coughed immediately, spitting out a mix of blood and dirt. She had lost a front tooth after a long struggle.

"You fuckin' mad arsehole, let me go," she ranted, after she had screamed her lungs out.

Shane shook his head at her, "No, no. Don't make things worse, Daisy. Please don't."

"No one hears you. You can scream as much as you bloody like, you stupid bitch," said a low gruff voice.

Shane tried desperately to twist his head, to look at their attacker but they were standing high, just out of his peripheral vision.

Daisy tried to roll onto her stomach and push up her body on her knees, but the butt of a riffle rained down on her head and she fell back onto her side. Her eyes were still open, but she was obviously dazed and further injured. Her long wavy brown hair sprayed over her face, some of it covered in bubbles of red blood spewing forth from her mouth. She wasn't talking anymore, her throat just making horrible gargling noises. Shane winched and tested the rope drawn tight and entwined over his wrists.

"Please, don't hurt her," Shane begged, eyes wide. "I never told her anything. She doesn't know anything."

"Okay. Righto. Just tell us what I need to know. And all will be okay."

"Please. Leave her alone. Leave her out of this. She doesn't know anything, okay?"

Their attacker stepped closer and roughly grabbed Shane's lank long hair and pulled him up by it. He was dragged to stand on his bare feet which made him cry out in excruciating pain, as the prickles dug in even deeper. Shoved roughly forward, he shuffled in his bound condition, heading in the direction of the kombi van, which stood on the perimeter of the clearing, in the shade of a giant blue gum, it's back wheels still planted on a partial dirt track. When he was too slow, he was dragged forward, his feet sliding across the hard ground.

Daisy was left behind on her bloody patch of earth, appearing to be lifeless except for her struggles to breathe.

Shane was pushed roughly to the back tailgate of the kombi van. They proceeded to punch him hard in his stomach. He dropped to his knees, doubled over in pain.

"Open it. Show me where it's stashed."

"Wh-what are you talking about?" Shane nervously asked, looking up at his attacker. He caught just a fleeting glimpse of a pair of cold black eyes peering over a black silk scarf hiding the lower features of their face.

"Hey boy, keep your bloody peepers down," the voice snarled at him.

Shane obeyed his command.

"You know. Where's the money? I'm not deaf and stupid. I heard you talking about the thousands you got stashed away. In your van."

"I don't understand."

He was cut off as a clenched ball of a fist knocked him down, back onto his knees, "I know what you fuckin' said. You said it's hidden away. Even she doesn't know about it, you said. Just show me where the money fuckin' is, and I'll let you go."

Shane looked over his shoulder to Daisy and repeated, "You will let us go?"

"Sure, mate. Give you my word. All I want is your stash of money."

He got back unsteadily to his feet, his hands were freed and he unlocked the side door. It slid open easily. Their assailant followed him inside the van, the rifle poking his ribs.

Shane's bloodied right hand felt under the mattress, and he took out a small metal box. Then he found the secret spot he had concealed the key. He gave it up.

Their assailant dropped the rifle a little as they opened the small metal box. They counted out the folded notes aloud and looked up at Shane's back after they were satisfied.

"Good job. Looks like you were bloody right. Thirty thousand dollars, you said."

"Take it all. Now please. Let us go."

They stepped back and lowered the rifle. But then the rifle was lifted up to the back of Shane's head, "No bloody way."

The rifle went off with a resounding blast. Birds noisily took flight from their roosting positions in the tree canopies in all directions, including a flock of noisy galahs. Fragments of blood and bone splattered across the interior walls of the van. The assailant then turned on their heel and headed in the direction of Daisy to finish the job they had come to do. They stopped suddenly in their tracks. They whistled out a signature tune, and more footsteps could be heard coming through the thick underbrush.

"She's all yours, mate. You can finish up the Daisy bird for us."

****

Raquel Willaston was busy loading up the dishwasher in Bette and Duncan's blackwood kitchen, getting ready to bake a chocolate cake from scratch. The ingredients were already stretched out across the island bench. She had decided to surprise Phil Duncan. He had hinted on the phone to her earlier that he may come home later. This was her chance to show him her domestic skills and he had missed out on tasting her lemon cheesecake. They were still getting used to each other's idiocrasies in their new live-in situation. She had come to learn that Duncan was a steadfast man of routine, the polar opposite of Phil Proctor. Whereas Proctor would easily drop things and go with the flow, Duncan had his day meticulously planned. When he got a sudden phone call from his office, he seemed out of sorts but altered his workday with no complaints. Privately, he liked order and routine.

He still kept his favourite wedding photograph with Bette on the bedside table. He was beaming behind her on the church steps, his arms holding her small waist as she stood there, in profile. But Raquel accepted it, understanding that it was part of his grieving process. She missed her good friend too.

While she missed Bette, she wanted to feel a part of Duncan's new life. She had decided to stamp her own personality and style to their home. She had already spent the last couple of days moving around the lounge room furniture to her own taste. She had ordered a new dining room suite with twelve chairs, which had been delivered that same afternoon. She had planned to entertain family and their friends more often, and Bette's basic six-chair setting wasn't going to cut it.

As she stood up, the dishwasher fully loaded, she heard the front doorbell ring. She had opened the flour bag a bit earlier and some of it already had covered her hands. She dusted it off on her black apron and walked through the lounge room with its large arched windows, bordered with swathes of deep red velvet curtain. She grimaced as she passed through, the opulent traditional look was not really her thing.

She swung the front door wide open to greet her tall policeman son.

Steve beamed at her, looking smart and neat in his dark navy uniform.

"Hey, Raquel, just passing by. Thought I'd say hello. And here's your paper."

"Great. Come in, come in," she moved quickly aside so he could breeze in and took the newspaper out of his grip, "I was about to start cooking, so good timing."

He gave her his standard lop-sided smile, "What? You never ever cook."

"Yes, I do. Not very often. But I'm in the mood today."

She walked back towards the kitchen, and he dutifully followed her.

He flicked his eyes around the lounge room as they walked through, "Have you moved things around in here?" He asked her, brushing his wavy brown hair back from his forehead. As he got older, his auburn hair had noticeably darkened.

She turned and smiled up at him, "Yes, I swapped the couch and armchairs around, to give us more space to move around. I think it looks better. What do you think?"

"I think…Phil might not agree with you. It was his space, you know. He told me he likes to work on his investigations in this room."

"I only swapped the furniture around. It's not a big change, honey."

She took off the apron to reveal her favourite leopard print maxi dress.

"You're suddenly a minimalist? Our home is still full of boxes piled about this high," he said, gesturing to his neck.

"I felt inspired."

"But what's this? I don't remember seeing this before," he stepped into the formal dining room, noticing the new stone and glass top dining table with twelve white leather chairs.

"Yeah. It's brand new. I just bought it. Very fancy, isn't it? Seats twelve people."

"Wow. I had no idea you even knew twelve people in town," he smirked.

She made a face.

Steve twirled his hat in his hands and asked. "Wow. You've bought more stuff to add to all the stuff you've got already. So, does Phil know about this?"

"Well, no. Not yet. The other dining table was drab and small. I know he'll love this one. You never saw his townhouse in Adelaide. This was the sort of furniture he had there. He's into all this modern stuff."

He knitted his eyebrows, "You saw his house in Adelaide?"

She waved her hand and shook her head, "Sorry, I meant to say that I saw photos of his townhouse on his mobile phone once. Yeah, he showed me photos."

She looked down briefly, thinking about her little white lie. She had never told him how she had met Duncan on a bad date before the death of the homeless man, the start of the infamous Brumby Flat murders.

Steve nodded his head and leaned against a dining chair, "It's lovely. But he doesn't seem like a person who likes so much 'change' in his life. He seems really conservative. Maybe you should ask him first, before doing any more work around the place. He lived with your best friend for a while. Maybe he liked her style more."

She heaved a sigh and sat down at the new dining table, "You think I'm being selfish?"

"Look. You're my mother. You've always been selfish. But that's part of your charm, to me. I admit. I am not really happy with this new relationship of yours. I wasn't mad keen on your bloody cowboy silo painter either. But when it comes to Detective Phil Duncan…I think you might be overdoing it. It's his home after all. He's not your Proctor guy. It's Duncan you're dealing with, who's obsessed with details and thinks about serious shit in his head all the time. I don't want to see the two of you fight. Maybe next time, you should wait and include him first in your plans before you do any more stuff around here."

She raised her eyebrows, "Okay. You're right. I get that."

Steve nodded and turned on his heel to leave, "Good. My job is done."

She turned over the paper to read the headline and gasped, "Oh, my god. Did you see this? 'Bodies found in park near Murder Town'. Unbelievable. The national park is like over fifty kms away from Brumby Flat. So close. Not."

Steve was tight-lipped and nodded his acknowledgement. He placed his hand on the front door handle but stopped in his tracks, "Oh, I nearly forgot. I stopped at the post office and some boxes came in for the Raindrops Shop. The label says whips, chaps and spurs?"

Raquel raised an eyebrow and then exclaimed, "Yep. That would be Bette's last order. Great. Half the town's been waiting for chaps, whips, spurs."

"God knows why," Steve remarked with a lopsided smile, scratching the back of his head, "Anyway. I've got some work to do. I can't discuss it with you."

"Of course. You never do. And that's okay, I get that. But I am super excited to be with him. Phil Duncan's like this breath of fresh air. You know?"

She followed her son to the front door.

Steve laughed and shrugged his shoulders, "Hey, I bet he is. But I don't want to know about it."

"And how's your new big romance going?" She leaned forward and nudged his ribs with her elbow.

"Kimberley? Oh yeah, she's great. She's the complete package. I've been invited to a big family barbeque. I will meet all her uncles and aunties. And her weird brother again. But I don't mind that at all."

"Oh good. Well, I'd better return to my cake. It won't bake itself."

Chapter Three

A new decade had dawned. Shane was enthusiastically stomping his feet to the beat of the blues band which had recently taken the makeshift stage. He was encircled by fellow music lovers who were standing around, in groups or pairs mainly, swaying to the rhythm. Some of the crowd were pleasantly drunk or high on something. He shook his thick mane of shoulder length light brown hair, which fell over his eyes at times and waved a clenched hand in the air. He was enjoying every minute of the local folk music festival in the middle of a lush national park. In his other hand, he held a joint, taking great care with it, as if it was a commodity in short supply.

For a moment, he shifted his focus. He craned his neck, looking out for his Daisy. He had downed a couple of beers real fast, so he was feeling a bit lightheaded. He thought he saw her a couple of times, but there were a few girls around who looked exactly like her from behind. They too had long wavy brown hair down to their waists and were wearing cropped jean shorts and t-shirts.

Finally, he saw her emerging from the music tent, carrying a new record under her arm. He waved and yelled her name out. She twisted her head and lowered her aviator sunglasses to reveal her bright blue eyes. Then she saw Shane and waved back excitedly. Shane burst into a sprint to reach her.

"Hey," he said, taking a sharp intake of breath when he caught up with her. He never got sick of her company. She was a free spirit, much like himself. He couldn't help admiring her curvy body and he was captivated by her large doe-like eyes. She had an unusual heart shaped face with a pert nose, and when she smiled, she had a noticeable toothy gap. She only wore a little eye makeup. She was a naturally beautiful girl.

"Hey, Shane. Check out what I got? My favourite band's new album."

He nodded, "Oh wow. Fantastic. This is some festive, hey. Met some cool guys. I've invited them to join us later. Back at our van."

Daisy could not attempt to disguise her frown, "Why? Shane, no. We don't have enough money to entertain other people, do we? I don't want us to be broke and stuck here after the show's long gone and over."

"It's alright. They will bring their own stuff over. And they got some of this," he raised his joint and drew on what was left of it, "Come on, Daisy. They seem to be real decent people."

She tossed her flowing hair over one shoulder, "Yeah, okay. I guess it's okay. But we offer them nothing to eat. We've only got enough cans of food for another week. I'll have to make some more jewellery to sell on the road. We need petrol money too."

"We can sell your jewellery right here."

"No. I have a bead necklace I want to show to the roadhouse lady. She bought one from me yesterday. She paid me a good price. I'm heading there now."

"Okay. I'll come too."

It was a good fifteen-minute brisk walk down the dirt trail to the roadhouse.

As they walked along the trail, she looked back over her shoulder a couple of times anxiously, certain she could hear sounds, like someone was walking behind them, but she did not see anyone. Then she would flick her eyes to look briefly at Shane. She was happy that he had come with her. There were a few people off their faces at the festival and these were the sorts she worried about being too close to.

When they made it to the roadhouse, they noticed it was unusually quiet. Every other time they had come up, there were usually people hanging around. Daisy opened the front door with Shane right behind her. The little alert bells tingled announcing their entry and the proprietor emerged from the kitchen, wiping her wet hands on a clean tea towel. Mabel was dealing with the arrival of the folk music festival on her front doorstep as best as she could. Not well prepared, she had been forced to improvise. She ordered extra soft drinks and cartons of chocolate bars by phone and the supplies fortunately arrived the same day. Then she had to deal with the fact that her sense of dress was too conservative for the youngsters who arrived in their carloads. She had let down her salt and pepper hair for a change and bought herself a rockstar emblazoned t-shirt from a stall holder. She had also bought a cheap string of colourful beads from one of the festival faithful.

She stepped forward to the counter, her palms flat on it and waited for the young couple to speak to her. Shane looked like he was about to run off any minute, while Daisy stuck a thumb in the loop of her low-slung shorts and stood firm, looking carefully over the neat shelves of confectionery.

"Howdy. And what can I do for you?" Mabel asked, her English clipped by her Irish phrasing.

"Hey. Hi again. I came by to show you a new necklace I've made. Made it last night I wondered if I could leave it here, in your shop to sell."

She juggled her new record into her other hand, as she removed it from her back pocket to reveal small fine beads fashioned with a large blue aqua pendant as it's centre piece. It wasn't anything special or very unusual, but Mabel knew the girl had spent time and great care creating it.

"Why, isn't that a lovely piece?"

Mabel studied Daisy hard with her experienced eye. She knew the young woman had a day-to-day struggle with life on the wide-open road.

"It's way too lovely to leave here."

Daisy's heart sank.

Mabel took a breath. Making her decision, she pressed down the key to open her till, and handed the girl a crisp twenty dollar note.

"Of course, I'll have to buy your necklace," she said with a slight smile and a sly wink.

"Wow, twenty dollars. Wow, thank you."

"And, my dear, you can help yourself to a chocolate bar too."

"Wow, thank you again."

Mabel nodded with kind eyes, as Daisy carefully placed the necklace into her outstretched hands.

Daisy then snatched up her favourite chocolate from the big selection and skipped out, Shane racing straight after her. He was just as excited by the sale, as she was.

"Wow. I didn't expect the old lady to do that. Look, we got twenty dollars. She only paid me five for the other necklace."

She proudly waved the note and then tucked it back into her shorts front pocket. They half ran and laughed as they started down the dirt trail to the clearing where the festival was being held.

"We could go back and get some food for everyone tonight," Shane suggested.

Daisy turned to him, walking backwards confidently, "No. They can bloody well bring their own. With this money, I really want to go back and pick up Byron. I mean we missed the boat to Tibet anyway. I wanna go back. I wanna get our son back."

She stopped walking and a solitary tear ran down her right cheek. Shane saw it and came up close to her and with his outstretched hand, he wiped it gently away.

"Sorry, Daisy. Yeah, you're right. We need to go back. Of course. We will. I promise you, when the festival ends tomorrow, we'll fill up the van and just head off. I miss Byron too."

Suddenly, they heard a noise coming from the left side, between the trees and thick scrubs. Daisy nervously crossed her arms over her chest and clutched her arms tight. She had tucked the record under her arm.

"Bloody hell. What was that? Did you hear that?" She took a step forward and whispered near Shane's ear, "Do you think someone is following us?"

He smiled and brushed her hair away from her face, "Nah. It's probably a 'roo. But we should get moving again."

She agreed and firmly slipped her hand into his. They walked on with a renewed sense of urgency. Five minutes along the trail and they heard a sound again. Daisy stopped and turned, sweeping her eyes nervously around them.

"There. I heard it again. I'm sure we are not alone."

Shane rolled his shoulders and dismissed her thoughts, "Daisy. You really are imagining things."

Just as he finished his sentence, a large shadow barrelled out of the bushes, and came at them both with lightning speed. There was no time for either of them to react. Both Daisy and Shane were felled with swift singular blows to their heads. They crashed onto the dirt rendered unconscious, with their attacker standing over where they lay, brandishing a rifle.

One by one, the young couple were dragged into the bushes to their predetermined fate.

****

Duncan knocked on his own front door for a couple of times. After waiting patiently for two minutes, he fished his house keys out of his trouser pocket. He unlocked his own front door and walked straight in.

"Hey, I'm back, hello," he yelled out. Still no reply came. He was used to Raquel being there to greet him and running into his arms. This afternoon, it was different. He felt uneasy and unsettled. It didn't help when he wandered around the back of the house and found dog poo all over the half court tennis court.

He threw his favourite tan jacket down to his left, but it fell straight onto the terracotta tiled floor. He stopped in his tracks and turned back, with a puzzled expression on his face. He remembered there was a chair in the corner, but it had mysteriously vanished. His intense blue eyes scanned the entrance hall around him.

His feet were planted firmly still, as he noted the not-so-subtle changes.

He heard Raquel pad in her bare feet across the polished timber floor in the dining room adjacent. She appeared wearing her red check Western shirt and denim skirt.

"Hello. Glad you're back," she smiled broadly and rushed forward to embrace him warmly, but he stepped backwards and then sideways, out of her reach. He glared back at her over the rims of his eyeglasses.

"What's wrong?" She asked, noticing his bristling mood. She stopped and dropped her arms to her sides.

"What *are* you doing?"

"What do you mean?"

"I came home to this. The chair that was here is magically gone and my good jacket's now on the floor. What have you done with my furniture?"

She bit down on her bottom lip, "Well, you did say I can make it my home. I just redecorated it a little bit," she replied, her voice trailing off.

"Redecorate, okay. I can understand that concept. But I didn't say you could get rid of any furniture. This is mainly Bette's stuff. I don't recognise that dining table over there and where the fuck's my goddamn chair gone? I did not give you permission to run riot in our home."

She placed her hands on her hips, "Phil. That's unfair. I haven't run riot. I only changed a few things. I'm very sorry about your chair. I had no idea how attached you were to it."

"Well, there you go. Now you know. I liked that chair."

She folded her arms across her chest and said in a low voice, "I get it now. I can return the chair. I just put it in the family room out the back, okay?"

"And," he added, his voice raised a notch more, "your bloody dog's gone and pooed all over the tennis court again."

Her hazel eyes had started to tear up, so she turned her face away. She was determined not to show him how much he had hurt her. She even attempted to walk away, but Duncan lurched forward and roughly grabbed her arm.

"Wait. Wait. Hold it," he had lowered his own voice, and turned her around now with a gentle, more restrained touch, "I'm sorry about my outburst just now. You're perfectly right. I said go ahead, make changes. It's my fault, completely. I didn't want to upset you, but I guess…Bette's death is still really raw to me. I still see a lot of her in this house, obviously. It just sort of shocked me, these little changes you've made. And yes, I liked the chair."

Raquel nodded her head, her eyes looking directly at the floor, "I'm sorry too. I don't think I thought about your feelings enough. You love your work, don't you? I haven't been very considerate, have I?"

He smiled slightly but said nothing in response.

"So? How was your day?"

He looked down too and she then realised he was overwhelmed by his emotions and perhaps overcome by shocking thoughts.

"Not a good one. But at least I know what became of my parents. I tried to call you earlier. I needed to talk."

She stepped forward, frowning, "Sorry, I was baking a cake when you called. I was up to my elbows in flour and food stuff."

"Okay. To a degree, I know something now. Forensics' have formally identified them to the remains which were found in the national park."

"I'm very sorry Phil."

He waved his hand in a dismissive gesture and turned his head to the right, avoiding her sad hazel eyes, "It's okay. Let's not go there right now. I have spent the last two days, being upset and thinking about them a lot. I wish I could remember them better. My mother, I remember she had curly dark hair. She played the guitar, you know. I don't remember my father, except that he was tall. And he was kind to me."

"If you need to talk about it."

Duncan stepped forward and tenderly pressed his forefinger against her soft lips.

"It's okay. I'm good now. Ah yes, and your son had a great idea too. He phoned me earlier. He's invited us all to go camping at the park. Did he ask you too?"

Raquel immediately screwed up her nose and laughed heartily, "I am not a camping type person. Don't expect me to come along. Camping's not my thing."

"Really? It's a 'No' straight away? You don't want to think it over? There'll be your son, his girlfriend, my new partner and the two of us."

She shook her head firmly.

"Right. I was looking forward to camping with you. But I know what will cheer me up. Why don't I put you to bed?"

She checked her wristwatch, "A bit early. It's only two o'clock. Oh."

It dawned on her what he meant. He grabbed her arm gently and directed her towards the narrow staircase. He lifted the palm of her right hand and placed it firmly against his heaving chest.

"Can you feel my heart beating fast?" He said in a low, soft voice.

She nodded her head, its frenetic pulse exciting her.

"Every time I am with you, this is how I honestly feel."

She stared up into his eyes, wanting to bring up the subject of Geena Henderson's surprise appearance at the back door but she knew he didn't need to be upset further after learning about his parents' horrible fate.

He suddenly clasped her against his chest and groin, and he kissed her lips hard, with a sense of urgency. His erection which pressed up in the fabric of his trousers told her all she needed to know. She breathed in his lust and the lingering smell of his cheap cologne. She hadn't expected the sexual attention so soon after his return, but she wasn't about to complain about it either. She willingly responded to all his moves and did not reject his hard and insistent kisses when they came. He was not the gentle, considered lover that had been Proctor's signature style. She didn't mind that he was different. She was starting to accept his intensity, which she assumed was a direct result of his work.

"Come on," he stopped and very firmly took her hand. He pulled her up the narrow stairs to the bedroom they shared.

Not wasting any time, he started to unbutton her western shirt. She reached for his shirt and started to do the same.

His hands reached around her and with a gentle touch, he glided his fingertips up and across her back. She closed her hazel eyes, enjoying his touch and then a memory of Proctor came back to her. She saw him standing in front of her, with only his cowboy hat strategically covering his dignity. She opened her eyes and the image disappeared.

She cried out, "Phil," at that precise moment, but fortunately, Duncan shared the same name, so he was none the wiser for it. In response, he leaned in closer and unfastened her bra. He very tenderly kissed the top curve of her left shoulder and then cupped his hand around her breast. He proceeded to blow and then suck hard on her erect nipple. She closed her eyes again, and this time, instead of dreaming of Proctor, she imagined he was actually physically there, seducing her. Not Duncan. She felt her skirt being unzipped and pulled down. Then a hand firmly parted her thighs slightly and a probing finger was slipped effortlessly into her vagina. Soon it was followed by another finger. Thrusting his fingers in and out, her vagina was soon wet and warm. She closed her eyes and felt a tingling sensation all over her body. Three fingers thrust inside her and twisted, and she audibly gasped.

She called his name out again, and Duncan took it as a favourable acknowledgement of his actions.

He suddenly gripped her naked waist, half lifted her body and stretched her out on his bed. Her hair was fanned across her face as she lay on her back, her arms laid taunt above her head. He unzipped his trousers and lay on his side next to her, his fingers still swirling inside her. Eyes closed, she moaned and shifted the positioning of her legs, now taking in four of his fingers. Finally, he withdrew his fingers altogether and pulled out his hard penis. He pulled her hips sideways and teased her vagina lips with the head of his penis before thrusting it in deep. He removed himself slowly and then proceeded to go down on her with his flicking, pointy tongue on her clitoris until she came, screaming his name and with her body shuddering like a runaway train. As she lay back, her erratic breathing starting to steady, Duncan easily slipped his hard penis inside her again. He thrust harder and faster. Finally, he gritted his teeth and groaned in ecstasy as he let his load explode within her. Then he kissed her very firmly and held her in his arms.

A good hour passed before Duncan began to make passionate love to her a second time. Afterwards, they spent the rest of the afternoon, locked together in an intimate embrace, eventually drifting off to sleep.

Raquel was wide awake long before Duncan, but she was happy to lay there quietly enfolded within his warm arms. As much as she was trying to move on and leave the recent past behind her, her head was swimming with random thoughts. Memories of being with Proctor still invaded her head space. While she cared deeply for Phil Duncan, she could still visualise Proctor easily. She even remembered the touch of his skin on her skin. The images and sensory triggers of her ex-lover were proving difficult to completely erase. She was lying in bed with one man and thinking non-stop about another far, far away.

Chapter Four

Duncan squinted and then shielded his eyes from the intense sun glare as he watched the four-wheel drive monster vehicle navigate and careen through the rough terrain and pull to a jerky stop right in front of him. He noted that the precision parking just missed rolling over his left pinkie toe. He was casually dressed in his pinstripe shirt with his best tan trousers to check out the national park. He was not expecting to do any real bushwalking.

Sullivan O'Grady hopped out, looking handsome, smooth and confident in his freshly starched park ranger uniform. He wore it with a few lose buttons, which showed off his perfectly tanned chest. He looked quite comfortable in his cargo pants. His days working in real estate were well and truly behind him and he seemed blissfully happy with his new job.

His sandy hair had a natural curl, his face was masculine perfection in its symmetry and his golden-brown eyes sparkled with undeniable charm. Duncan knew he himself came off as second best in O'Grady's alpha male presence.

He put out his hand to shake Duncan's.

"Hey, mate," he said with a tight-lipped smile, his mind racing back to an unpleasant memory when he was under suspicion for an attempted murder.

Duncan squared off, "Hope there's no hard feelings. We all had a job to do back then."

Sullivan waved his hand, "It's okay. Water under the bridge. So, you want to see my backyard today? It's pretty impressive, my office with a massive view. Mate, I just love it out here."

"Yeah, you're a lucky man."

"Only bad thing is hearing about these bloody murders. Before my time but it will affect numbers coming out to Beecham's. I am wondering if plans for the Folk Festival anniversary will be rooted."

"You're talking about my parents actually," Duncan said with a heavy sigh.

"Oh, mate. I'm sorry. I wasn't thinking too clearly."

Duncan made a clicking sound in the hollow of his cheek and brushed off Sullivan's hasty words.

"It's okay. But I think the folk festival will go ahead. The promoters have already put up a lot of signage about the place. Some people would come up here anyway, it's probably a morbid fascination for them."

"You're quite right, mate. Anyway, let's get started. There's lots to see in the park."

Duncan carried his notebook in the back pocket of his trousers. He pulled it out and made notes when he had cause to. Sullivan had only recently secured the job of park ranger, but he had already mapped out the territory and knew the best camping spots and where the park natural features were. They drove through a few winding dirt tracks, and he showed the detective the creek which meandered through the park, several natural rock outcrops and pointed out the directions for the various walking trails.

"That's the best one. Goes for kilometres and over some nice terrain," Sullivan pointed to his left, and Duncan had to crane his neck over the dashboard to see. He noted that it was positioned close to a carpark with toilet facilities further down. He quickly scrawled some notes.

"It was also the trail that led to the kombi van. The scrub was pretty dense around there. Lucky to find it," he added.

For the tenth time during their drive, Sullivan's mobile phone rang. He looked down at the number, but he didn't answer it again.

"Who is that? Why don't you ever answer it? They keep on calling you."

The park ranger grimaced and shook his head, his elbow sticking out over the open window of the vehicle, "It's okay, mate. Just my last girlfriend. She's still obsessed with me, if you know what I mean. She reckons I'm good in bed. I have a natural gift, you see. I just know what a woman wants from a bloke like me. And I give it freely."

It was too much information for Duncan who just made a face and shifted uneasily in his car seat.

Eventually, Sullivan O'Grady turned the four-wheel drive vehicle onto the dirt track leading up to the secluded ranger's cabin. It was the roughest ride yet for Duncan, the car splattering and jolting over the many potholes along the way. The wheels seemed to rotate in different directions and Duncan was forced to hold onto the hand grip above his head. When they finally pulled up at the cabin which was actually an old tin shack, he was impressed by the size of the place.

As they stepped out of the vehicle, Sullivan indicated a thumb towards the ground.

"Watch out for the kangaroo poo. It's all over the ground. They don't hold back around here."

Outwardly, the building was weathered and neglected, but when Sullivan unlocked the side door, Duncan stood on the solid hardwood timber floor and marvelled at the length of the scout hall inside.

"Wow, big place," he remarked.

"The scouts use this campsite quite a bit, but since the recent discovery of bodies…well, they've taken up camp elsewhere. Our rangers' office is here at the back. It's kind of a small space but it's still serviceable."

"Okay. Show me."

He followed Sullivan through the narrow kitchen, noting the evident signs of mouse droppings on the empty benches. He unlocked the door to the room on the left. They entered the office and Duncan whirled around the middle of it, noting the park maps blue-tacked to the asbestos walls. There were photographs of the surrounding nature too, pinned haphazardly all over the old pinboard.

On the built-in corner desk, there was a working telephone, spare binoculars, a dusty plastic sleeve folder and an old photo album overflowing with pictures.

"What's this?" He tapped his forefinger on the photo album.

"Well, yeah, that might be of interest to you, detective. It's like a history of the park. There're photos of all the park rangers who have worked here over the years. Most of them. Some pictures may be missing."

He slowly turned over the pages. Some were stuck to each other, and older photos had faded to tinted smudges. Fortunately, there was a flourish of writing under some, complete with names, events and years.

"Do any of the rangers still live around here?" Duncan asked, flicking through the last couple of pages.

Sullivan scratched his nose, and shifted his weight to his tanned right leg, "I think maybe three are still here. Two are dead. The best one to talk to is Old Chook. He's the living oracle around here. He was the ranger over forty years ago. And then, he came back to it when he had to replace one of the park rangers who came after him. Yeah. This one was a real crazy guy apparently. Scared some of the tourists away."

"Right. Is his picture in the book? The scary one."

"I don't think so, mate. I believe he only lasted five months in the job. There'd be information kept at the head office about him. I guess you'll need access to these old files?"

"Definitely. Maybe it will help our investigations. And I must meet Old Chook."

"He's easy to find. Nearly every other day, he's sitting at the Batty. Hangs out there for a drink and a chat. He knows this region and all its stories like the back of his wrinkled hand."

Duncan smirked. Old Chook was exactly the person he needed to question.

Sullivan frowned and lifted his hand.

"Do you hear that?" He said in a low voice, "Trail bikes in the park again. I'm forever telling them off. I'll drop you back at your car."

****

It was nine o'clock in the morning and a fine mist had settled across the Batty Roadhouse and the surrounding bushland. The gloom was slowly starting to lift as clouds parted in the sky above to reveal the first shards of sunlight. A lone, skinny figure trudged across the hard ground, making their way to the roadhouse.

Old 'Chook' was something of a regular fixture around the district. No one knew exactly how old he actually was, but he still lived in the same farmhouse he was born in. One of nine children born to Scottish immigrants, he was the last one still alive and the only one of them who had stayed home. Aside from a brief trip to Adelaide decades ago, he had never strayed far from the district.

Over the years, he had served the local community in various capacities. He had worked in the Batty, as a local firefighter, a sheep shearer, a farmhand and a park ranger. Although officially retired, he still did odd jobs for locals, and he was the first person to call if there was a snake to catch. His closest neighbour was Barb Hillman and they always helped each other out.

Advancing age had well and truly slowed him down. His shoulders were now hunched over, his face was heavily lined and painfully thin. His jowls hung slack under his stubbly grey chin. He was average in height, but he was getting skinnier and had to hitch up his trousers with suspenders. His white shirt was well-worn, oversized on his slight frame and yellowed with age. But he was old school, so he preferred to hold onto what was familiar, rather than replace. Even a badly chipped teacup, a plate with a crack or a tea towel with a tear in it was worth holding onto.

He walked briskly through the sliding glass doors of the Batty and waved his bony hand to Banksia who nodded her head in return. He could see she was busy sorting the mail, so Chook went direct to his favourite stool and plonked himself down. He folded his skinny arms over the countertop, waiting patiently for Banksia to finish her work, so he could order his breakfast. Every second day, he came to the Batty for a cooked breakfast.

When she finally finished the sorting, she walked over to him behind the counter and said, "Chook. Good to see you. The city detectives were looking for you this morning. I think they'll be back shortly."

"What do they want from an old fella like me?" He retorted, pulling a disagreeable face. He had left his false teeth at home, so his face appeared longer than usual, and his words came out mumbled.

"No idea. Do you want a coffee while you wait?"

"Is it free?"

"No. Unless you're happy with instant coffee."

He shrugged his shoulders, "I'll just have one of those, mate. That'll do me. I like the simple pleasures. A splash of milk in it too, thanks."

She nodded her head, knowing him well enough. She boiled the kettle and made them both a strong instant.

Chook was grateful as he clutched his mug of steaming hot coffee. Just as he had taken two quick gulps of his rare free drink, the detectives arrived through the glass sliding doors. Both were wearing their best suits, although Duncan had his tan jacket draped in a casual fashion over his outstretched left arm.

"Chook, is it?" Rich was the first to speak, proffering his hand to shake the old man's.

"Yeah, it's definitely me. Don't wear my name out. What can I do you for?"

Duncan cleared his throat and took over, "I'm Senior Detective Duncan and this is Detective Bottrell. We've been told that you've lived in the district for quite some time, and you know everyone around the place."

"Lived? Mate. Born and raised more likely. Yeah. I'm on first name terms with the cockroaches here too."

"And you served as a park ranger?"

He nodded his grey head, "Yep, sure was. On two occasions, I was the ranger."

Duncan flashed up his credentials and continued, "As you know, we are investigating the murders in the park. Thought you might be able to talk to us about your job back then and what you observed maybe in the last thirty odd years."

"What? Suspicious stuff, you mean?"

Rich stretched the back of his neck, hands on hips, "Yeah, I guess. If you remember anything unusual. Something worth telling us about."

Old Chook rested his coffee mug back on the countertop and made a broad sweeping gesture with his right hand, "Beecham's Bridge, to my thinking, she's much like a lady. She's a bit proud and holds onto her secrets, but I have to be honest, detectives. I have been privy to some of them."

He told a deep breath before continuing, "Maybe we'll start from here. I was the park ranger for about six years the first time around. Oh god. That was about forty odd years ago.

Anyway, I left the job, and the next park ranger was Ryan Wayne Parsons. Well, now, he was a right scary bastard. Been dead a few years now, so you won't be able to get a word out of him. Died of a nasty brain tumour."

Duncan had his notebook open and made his ballpoint pen busy, "Scary? Why's that?" He asked.

"He didn't so much as talk to you, as bark at you. Ryan was an angry son of a bitch at the best of times. Blamed everyone, except himself for the loss of the family farm to the bank people. We understood that he had it hard for a while there. I told him to take up the ranger job, hoping it might straighten him out. But I don't think it did. He liked to carry his shotgun with him when he patrolled the park, and it concerned the tourists and locals alike. Sometimes, you heard him shoot off some rounds in there. He was always saying he was killing pesky rabbits. But the authorities didn't like that, and he only lasted a few months in the job. After that, he met Barb Hillman who became his partner. I think she sort of straightened him out a bit. At any rate, he calmed down a bit, which was a good thing."

"So, he lost the farm but still managed to live out here."

Chook nodded, "I believe Barb came into some money from her family. An inheritance she told me. She bought out his farm about thirty years ago and they lived there together, breeding cattle until he died about five years ago."

He continued, "The park ranger who came after Ryan, well, he was a bit of a funny character too. Not talkative. Unhelpful mug too. Tourists were always complaining. He's still living around here so it might be worth you talking to him, if he talks now to people. Bill…I've forgotten his last name. Anyway, he lives at the end of Beecham's Drive. You can't miss his yellow painted truck tyres at the front gate. The road's just on your left, after the hundred-kilometre zone."

Suddenly, his eyes narrowed as he looked off into the distance and he lowered his voice, "Shhh, here's Barb coming. We didn't really talk about Ryan."

Barb Hillman had strolled through the roadhouse sliding doors. She was tall and willowy in build but had a middle-aged spread waist which rolled over the top of her work jeans. She entered the shop singing a country tune and holding the tip of her battered and dusty western hat. Wearing no makeup, she had rosy cheeks, a ruddy complexion and fine lines had settled around her eyes and around her thin, wide mouth. A much deeper line ran down her right cheek to her strong square jawline. Her eyes were a fawny brown colour and she wore her long grey hair in a tightly drawn ponytail under her hat. There was a no-nonsense air about her.

She smiled at Chook and gave him a small wave. She noticed the two detectives and mouthed a quiet hello to them.

Rich cried out, "Hey, Barb Hillman."

She stopped her determined walk to the shop counter and spun around on her boot heel. With hands shoved in her jean's pockets, she came to a standstill in front of them.

"That's me. What's up?"

Rich showed his credentials, "I'm Detective Richard Bottrell and this is Senior Detective Phillip Duncan. We wanted to chat to you about the bodies found recently in the national park."

She raised an eyebrow, "It happened over thirty years ago, didn't it? Geez. I have probs remembering what happened a week ago," she said and chuckled.

"It's important to us. And not a laughing matter," Duncan interjected drily.

With the clarity of his words and strong voice, he got her complete attention and she studied him the longest under the shadow of her hat, "Yeah, it's a terrible business. But I don't know what I can add to help your investigations."

"Where were you at the time of the murders?"

She bit her bottom lip, "I have given it a thought lately. I think I had just arrived here at Beecham's, and I met the love of my life soon after. We moved into his farm and that was it. I don't remember anything else. We were devoted to each other for years until he got sick real bad."

"Where is the love of your life now?" Rich asked.

"Ryan? He passed away a few years ago. He had cancer, the terminal sort. But I keep on going. The farms' all mine now, you see."

"Righto. Do you remember seeing people hanging around after the big folk festival back then?"

Barb blinked slowly and shook her head, "Nah, mate. There were lots of people hanging around. A lot of people set up camp in the park for the festival. Sure, some stayed past the concert date but come on, we're talking, like, over thirty years ago, detectives. I don't remember faces or names. I'm sorry guys. Chook might remember more stuff."

Chook shrugged his bony shoulders and said, "Barb, I've already talked to them, about what I remembered."

She nodded her head, "You have? Well then. Good for you," she flashed a tight-lipped smile. "Sorry. I have nothing more to add to what you already know, detectives."

Chapter Five

Duncan had parked his car in the dirt and gravel carpark adjacent to the campground and he had parked crooked. He was running late, and he knew he had missed the planned bush walk. He recognised Rich's flash car and Raquel's Pontiac which told him that Steve Willaston had borrowed his mother's car again.

He looked around as he emerged from his car, impressed by the surrounding dense bushland and the pleasant buzz of wildlife. Sullivan had been right on the money. He had said it was a beautiful, isolated spot but still close to the track and toilet facilities. He stepped up to the tourist information billboard and noted the direction of the walking trail.

He wasn't dressed for camping. He had come straight from the Brumby Flat Police Station, after reading through some old crime reports linked to the park. He had teamed his best white shirt with his tan trousers. His polished tan leather dress shoes crunched on the gravel and fine red dust rose as he went to the back and opened the hatch door. He pulled out the tent swag and his esky of food and cold beer to share. He draped extra clothes he had brought along, carefully over his left arm. He had not camped outdoors since his young days travelling with his parents, so he didn't have any great expectations. Apart from purchasing a tent from a big retailer and borrowing an esky from a friend, which was the sum total of his camping preparations.

He locked his car and trudged down the crocked path towards the sound of animated voices which carried on the slight breeze.

"Hey, Phil," Steve yelled out his greeting, as the detective came into view, joining them in the small clearing. He put out his hand and gave him his trademark lopsided smile. Duncan shook his hand vigorously. Steve was out of his policeman's uniform for a change, embracing his top-to-toe black rockstar look.

Steve's impressive tent was already up, while Rich was still putting in the stakes for his into the hard ground, hammering at them with the heels of his best shoes. He was also peppering the air with a few choices swear words.

"Hey. Perfect place to camp."

"Love it. Mate, I have to introduce you to my girlfriend."

"Sure. I'll set up just here," he dropped the tent swag and rested the beer laden esky carefully on the ground. Duncan turned to look more closely at Steve's tent which looked like the Taj Mahal of tents.

Suddenly, a blonde head appeared, ducking under its entrance. As soon as she raised her pale grey-blue eyes and flashed her dimpled smile, Duncan audibly gasped. His eyes took in her youthful beauty and her slight but curvaceous frame. She was wearing a check shirt tied under her bustline and a pair of denim high waisted shorts.

When she smiled, her twenty something face lit up, like he was a glittering prize, which was, of course, all in his own mind. He stepped awkwardly backwards and fell over his own swag.

As he lay sprawled on his backside, with his eyeglasses askew on his nose, she giggled.

"Are you okay?" Steve lunged forward, thrusting his hand out, but Duncan was already bracing himself to stand up on his own.

"I'm right," he said in a sharp tone, followed with a throat clearing cough.

"Detective, this is Kimberley Jackson."

Duncan dusted his hands over his white shirt, still not thinking very clearly. He held out his right hand to shake hers. She gave him back a firm handshake. But he held her hand two seconds longer than he needed to, and he felt an electric charge pass through the tips of their fingers. He perceived that she had felt it too. Her eyes locked with his for longer than expected. Only Steve's voice short circuited their initial connection.

"Pity my mother couldn't make it."

Duncan reluctantly released her hand, "Hi, very nice to meet you. What's your story?'

She blushed a little, "I live in Brumby Flat. I'm a local firefighter too. I've heard everything about you, but I didn't think you'd be so funny."

Duncan smirked and inclined his head, "An element of surprise is important in my work."

Steve's face hovered into their peripheral line of vision, as he slipped an affectionate arm casually around Kimberley's shoulders and kissed her left cheek quickly. She smiled shyly and her dimple reappeared.

"Isn't she great? We'll let you get yourself organised."

He pulled her away and Duncan watched the smooth backs of her shapely legs. He only averted his admiring gaze when they sat down on their respective camp chairs.

He knelt down and unpacked the swag to start his tent assembly. Duncan struggled with his small tent which he had bought from a department store rather than from a specialist camping gear supplier. He had no idea how to go about it, but he knew what the end result had to look like. He studied the instruction sheet and placed parts on the ground, in the configuration shown. But it didn't help him very much.

After watching him battle it out alone for thirty minutes, Kimberley leaned across and nudged Steve gently in his ribs, "Maybe you should go and give him a hand. He's all thumbs you know. He's your superior, isn't he?"

Steve swallowed another gulp of beer and leaned towards her to whisper low in her ear, "Look, I have to be honest, but I'm not really comfortable with him being around. He's shacked up with my mother. Or she's shacked up with him. It happened quickly, before his dead wife's body was even cold in the ground."

"Oh, I didn't know."

"It's okay. I'm worried for Raquel because I think he's let her down a couple of times before."

Kimberley considered his barrage of words and exclaimed, "So what you're saying to me...he's a bit of player. Is that what you're saying?"

"Maybe. Yeah, okay. But I'll give him a hand in a minute. I'm not going to rush it."

When he still didn't move after five minutes, Kimberley pushed herself up out of her chair and decided to wander over to Duncan. He glanced up as she stood over him, trying hard to study her face rather than her crotch in those really tight denim shorts she had miraculously poured herself into.

"Need a hand?"

"Two are preferable."

She giggled again and squatted down. She glanced down at the instruction sheet and together they worked on the project. He kept looking at her under his eyelashes. He was trying hard not to stare at her crotch between her parted knees. It took her all of ten minutes to put most of the tent together.

"There you are," she said with a sense of undisguised triumph, standing up, her hands resting on her hips.

"Oh, is that it? It looks rather flat. It's not very roomy looking."

"It's just the sort of tent you crawl into, and you sleep in it. That was your plan tonight, wasn't it?"

"Oh, yes," he rolled his shoulders and enthusiastically nodded, "My only goal is to sleep. Just to sleep. Squashed up in this really tiny tent."

She smiled, blushed a little and walked back to sit with her Steve.

As the evening closed in, the four of them sat gathered around in their camp chairs, laughing, drinking and chatting. Rich had remembered to bring his portable camp lantern which was strategically placed in the centre. It provided just enough light to see each other's faces, distinguish silhouettes and to fish out refreshments from their nest of eskies.

"Oh, my god. Suddenly, I'm so bloody cold," Kimberley said, clutching her shivering arms, as a strong gust of cool air rustled the gumtree branches above them and whistled through the bushes.

"It's the gully winds coming through," Duncan remarked, clutching his beer.

"Ranger Sullivan mentioned it."

"Do you want my jacket, Kimie?" Steve piped up, "No wonder you're bloody cold, honey. You're wearing next to nothing."

"I've got my jumper here," Duncan offered.

Steve laughed and took another swig of his beer, "What the fuck! Only old guys wear jumpers."

Duncan smirked but felt put out by the comment, "I only took it with me because I heard about the gully winds. You're welcome to wear it. Keep you nice and warm."

He got up as he was sitting on it and tossed it to Kimberley. She grabbed it easily and immediately held the garment against her chest and left cheek.

"Wow. It's so warm," she said as she rolled the arms, and enthusiastically she pulled it over her head and adjusted it over the curvy contours of her body. He watched her as much as he could, without drawing suspicion.

Suddenly, Rich turned to look at his new partner Duncan in the cool light of the lantern.

"Hey. I'm sorry to hear about your wife, mate. Longmeil told me."

Duncan nodded his head a couple of times and said in a considered tone of voice, "Thank you. Our time together was cut way too short. But her best friend has supported me right through it."

"Nice."

"Yes, she lives with me now."

Rich had taken a gulp of his beer and nearly spat it all out, "Oh man. Look at you go. You've moved on already."

"He means he's gone and shacked up with my mother," Steve added sarcastically.

"It's not like that. I've had a few dark days. We've known each other for quite some time and Raquel's just a lovely, caring person. We have a strong understanding and a nice respect for each other."

"I'm sure you do," Steve looked at him darkly and Kimberley noticed the tension in the air.

"Hey, guess what? I saw my first koala today," she said brightly, managing to change the focus to Australian wildlife.

The group stayed up for another hour, before Steve finally raised his arms high in the night air and stretched, following it up with a big yawn.

"Well, Kimie. Let's go to bed."

She turned and smiled wistfully at him.

"Yeah. It's been a bit of a long day."

Rich straightened his suit jacket and turned to head off to his own tent, "Night, you two lovebirds. See you, Phil."

Alone in the clearing, Duncan stood up and stretched the knots out of his spine. He heaved a heavy sigh and replayed the entire day's events in his head. Not a lot had happened, but Steve's girlfriend had certainly turned his whole world upside down. He spied some movement from the corner of his eye. Suddenly, he saw Kimberley. She was standing right next to his arm, her breathing coming hard and fast.

"You'll want this back," she half whispered to him, and he watched mesmerised as she pulled the jumper quickly up and over her head. As it came off, her long blonde hair sprayed with static electricity across her shoulders and cheeks. He saw one pale breast jiggle and it very nearly slipped out of her tied up shirt. His intense blue eyes came to rest on her heaving left breast which curved seductively in the lantern's diminishing light. He was sure he could see the soft edges of a pink nipple peeping out. He was tempted to lean forward, closer to her and breathe her sexual essence in, but he resisted the primeval urge. Her pale blue eyes stared big and bright up at him. Then they retreated into the darkness of the night. Somehow, she had managed to slip his neatly folded jumper into his hands. He brought it up to his chest and briefly closed his eyes. He could still feel her bodily warmth and smell her lingering scents captured within the folds of his jumper.

He carried it back, folded it over once more and placed it gently inside his tent. Using his jumper as a pillow, he found himself dreaming of Kimberley Jackson all that night.

Chapter Six

Duncan woke up early the next morning and propped up on his elbows, he peered out of his small, squat tent. He had tried to keep her out of his head all night, but now she was standing right outside, in the flesh. Kimberley was an early riser too apparently, and as he peered out, she was stretched in the midst of a well-known yoga pose on top of her yoga mat. Her ash blonde hair shone bright in the first light of day, and the shards of sunlight had started to caress her curves. She was just a fraction taller than his deceased wife, and her curvy body reminded him of a goddess statue from ancient times. She was wearing a low-cut top with an intricate web strap crossover across her back, with shorts. He was strangely attracted to her. He felt connected in a way he had never experienced before. With Raquel Willaston, it was lust and familiarity, but this attraction to Kimberley was altogether something new. It was electrifying and unfathomable to him to clearly define.

He also had something of a monster erection which he was trying hard to control. He had to wait patiently for it to pass.

Eventually, he coughed loudly to clear his throat. He pushed himself forward with his elbows, rose up awkwardly from the entrance of his tent and stood up, wearing his lycra black long pants, his expensive wristwatch and nothing else. As he had anticipated. Kimberley did a double take, her eyes lingering momentarily on his crotch.

"Good morning," he said, in his strong clear voice.

"Morning," she replied brightly, returning to her new yoga pose.

"You're up pretty early," he remarked.

"I could say the same for you."

"Where's Steve and Richard?"

Kimberley half smiled and leaned into the yoga position further, "Steve's snoring away in there. I'm surprised you didn't hear him last night. And I think your detective mate, he drove away last night. His car's gone."

Duncan glanced at the spot where his partner had pitched his tent and realised the space was indeed empty.

"Oh well. Should we cook some breakfast?"

She shook her head, bent over and proceeded to roll up her yoga mat. As she did, Duncan adjusted his eyeglasses on the bridge of his nose and watched her well-shaped bottom bounce up and down in those tight shorts. Kimberley turned her head and caught him looking. She averted her eyes, stood up and straightened her back.

"I'm fine. I'm not really hungry."

"How about a quick bushwalk? I know of a good trail. The Park Ranger recommended it to me."

She regarded him under her wispy fringe, "Oh yeah? Why ever not? I'll just put on my hiking shoes."

She ducked her head into the tent she shared with Steve Willaston and Duncan crouched down and felt for his t-shirt inside his own. She had quickly changed. She emerged wearing a t-shirt and a pair of tight stretch jeans. A few moments later, he was leading her through some low-lying bushes and onto a small winding dirt trail. He wasn't confident he had found the correct path, but Sullivan had told him it was near the campsite, veering to the right.

They trudged through the bushland for a good twenty minutes when Kimberley tapped him lightly on his right shoulder, "Hey, detective. Do you even know where we are?"

"Of course, we just have to go a bit further. Some amazing views ahead. I promise you."

He turned back to the dirt path and kept walking. Kimberley followed but this time, they started to chat. They talked about the weather and some other general topics. They had walked for at least an hour, when they came across a small clearing. Duncan stopped, leaned his sweaty back against a tree and took a long swig from his water bottle. He offered her a drink, but she waved her hand.

Kimberley darted her light grey-blue eyes around the clearing and sat back on a large rock jutting from the ground, a fortunate find.

"Come on, detective. Are we lost? It sort of feels like we are," she asked him directly.

Duncan adjusted his eyeglasses and sighed, "Maybe. But I am sure we can find our way back. I just need a few minutes to think," he replied.

She crossed her arms and leaned forward, "I can't believe this. You've got us bloody lost. I left my mobile phone behind in the tent. Where's yours?"

He shrugged his shoulders and pointed a thumb back in the direction they had come from, "So did I. Chill. It's okay, we just go back the same way we came. Anyway, why don't we just talk for a while. It's such a beautiful morning. So? What's your story?"

She blinked a couple of times, "You asked me the same question last night. Right. You're kidding me. You got us lost, so you can question me? About murders here? I've never been to this park before."

"No, no. I mean, I just want to genuinely know more about you. If I may, Kimberley."

She studied his intense blue eyes which were firmly locked on hers.

"I am with Steve," she told him in a firm, factual tone of voice.

But Duncan was steadfast and chose to ignore her comment.

"I'm not asking you about Constable Willaston. I am trying to talk to you. Find out about you. I know Willaston well enough."

She broke their gaze and looked down at the ground, "There's not too much to tell. I am a firie, you know that already. I joined straight after my parents died in that fire which came through Brumby Flat a few years ago. I was hell mad, you know. Really angry that I had lost them."

Duncan nodded, "At least you had years to enjoy with your parents. Mine disappeared when I was still very young. They left me with my grandparents in Queensland and went off to Tibet. My grandparents actually raised me, put me through university."

"Oh, I'm sorry."

"Don't be. I was lucky. My grandparents adored me. It was like I was their son. I didn't think about my parents too much. I didn't know them long enough, in the scheme of things. They were supposed to have gone to Tibet, but they were found here recently, unearthed in the park. Their bodies were buried here for over thirty years, you know."

"Oh wow. Sorry to hear that. Yes, I read about it."

"Anyway, my anger also changed me. I became a homicide detective. I guess that was me dealing with things, as an angry young man. Right now, I am trying to mentally deal with these facts. It's very hard to process the fact that they were killed here, murdered. And in such a beautiful place too."

"I imagine so. But then, I can't put myself in your shoes. Murder is not in my experience. It's your truth which you must walk and accept, detective. We all have to accept our truths for ourselves."

Duncan raised an eyebrow and quietly acknowledged how wise she seemed for her age. Her observations impressed him, whenever they talked in depth. He had hung on her every word at last night's camp.

"Yes, it's very lovely here," she added, pausing to take in the natural sounds of the bush surrounding them. He watched a solitary tear trail down her left cheek but she quickly wiped it clean away. An awkward silence descended before she finally broke the spell.

"Can you hear that sound?"

He listened intently, but all he could hear was the chorus of birdsong and cicadas around them.

"It sounds like a creek. Must be fresh water close by."

She sprung from the rock and started walking in the direction of the trickling water sounds. Duncan followed as she disappeared into the underbrush and behind a group of spindly juvenile gumtrees.

When he finally saw her back and perfectly round buttocks clearly again, they were standing in front of a waterhole with a steady trickle of water cascading from boulders above the pool.

"Oh wow," she gasped, sweeping a hand over her blonde hair, "Isn't this a magic spot?"

The attractive dimple appeared again as she smiled. Duncan swallowed hard next to her and ventured a brief sideward glance at her profile. He drank in her rosy cheek, her generous pink budded lips and shiny forehead. He closed his eyes for a brief moment and imagined what kissing her would be like.

"Very beautiful," he said, nodding his head in agreement.

She turned her head briefly, and he quickly gazed forward again. He felt guilty looking at her, but he found it hard not to. His attraction to her was undeniably strong. He could feel his heart racing, ready to leap out of his chest and found it difficult to concentrate on anything else.

"You're so easy to read, Detective Duncan."

He smirked, "Please. Call me Phil."

"Phil. I know you like me. You look at me differently. Not the way Steve does."

"I'm not your Steve," he retorted, "and I'm sorry if I am making you feel uncomfortable."

She smiled shyly at him, "I wouldn't say that. You flatter me with your attention, but I am wondering if I would be just a trophy for you. A foolish, younger woman to conquer. Hey? Is that what you are really thinking?"

He looked at her direct with his intense blue eyes and said in a soft, candid tone, "Never that. Try and put your trust in me."

Kimberley tentatively stepped forward and leaned into him, her generous lips parted and quivering. She looked like she was about to tell him something. But she was standing far too close, which was an insufferable situation for him.

He made a quick decision. Duncan took a deep breath and blew out warm air as he bent over and enveloped her full lips with his mouth. For once, he was tender and considered his effect on her. She did not resist his touch and surrendered to his complete control. It was a soft, firm but needy kiss. With his right hand, his long tapering fingers smoothed her soft silken hair and curled a strand over one ear. When the slow kiss had finished, Kimberley broke free and raced towards the water hole, tugging her white t-shirt up over her head. Her ample breasts jiggled in her sports bra as she did, further taunting him.

"Last one in, has to pack up *all* the camping gear," she cried out.

Duncan raced after her, also grappling with his t-shirt and tossing it into the nearby bushes. He quickly set his eyeglasses down at the waters' edge. They both entered the water almost at the same time, still wearing their sneakers, pants and underwear. They laughed and playfully splashed a stream of water at each other. Kimberley then briefly slipped under the water and when she resurfaced, Duncan's face appeared close to her own. She giggled and flicked her wet hair back. He stood up in the shallow pool and held her chin up. She too stood in front of him, he pulled her up higher by grasping her waist. He began to twirl her slowly around in the chest deep dark water. They studied each other's eyes wordlessly.

After a while, he pressed his groin against hers. She gasped as she felt how hard he actually was.

"Phil," she said his name with an emotional intensity.

His return voice to her was gentle and his words sincere, "I can stop, if you want me to stop."

"Hey. Do you think there's anything under the water that we should worry about?" She practically whispered the words.

"Maybe eels, and just my dick," he twisted his lips in a wry smile.

She giggled and then, she began to breathe rapidly. In answer as to whether he should stop, very casually she unhooked her sports bra from the front. Her large, firm breasts were laid bare on the surface of the cool water, her nipples sharp and erect in his face. She placed her left arm around his wet shoulders to brace herself, and with her right hand she pushed down and freed his penis from his tight lycra pants. She quickly unzipped and pulled down her own stretch jeans underwater and kicked them off to float down to the waterhole floor.

He held her tight against him. and high in the water and greedily kissed her wet face all over. Ripples of water parted around their partially submerged bodies. Her breasts gently jiggled on the surface of the water and he teased the aureole encircling one of her hard pink nipples with his flicking, pointy tongue. Then he stopped to look deeply into her eyes.

"It's okay. Don't you dare stop now," she whispered, barely audible into his ear.

He suddenly picked her up in his arms and carried her out of the waterhole. She clasped her hands around his neck. He pushed her back up against a leaning tall old gumtree trunk next to the water's edge. The texture of the bark was rough against her soft skin, but she didn't care. She parted her bare thighs gently, twisted her wet cotton knickers out of the way and guided his hard penis inside of her. She gasped and tossed her head far back as he thrust his way deep into her. He thrust again and again, sending wave after wave of pleasure crashing through her body. The tension was building as he intensified his thrusting and then slowly drew his penis out to its tip and teased her vagina lips with it. Then he thrust down hard into her again. He tipped her pretty face upwards under her chin and kissed her deeply and tenderly as he very gently kneaded a pale breast with his free hand. His fingers tugged and teased her hard pink nipples. Her chest heaved in her excitement.

Finally, he reached a satisfying climax, crying out and adding his voice to the natural sounds of the bush. Kimberley felt a rush of warmth enter her. She let out a low moan of pleasure and kissed him back eagerly. He rubbed her clit with his wet forefinger until she too came. She trembled in his arms.

"Leave him," he said, his tongue rolling over her left earlobe, then her right. She shivered involuntarily at his light, seductive touch.

"And do what, Phil? What is that you expect me to do exactly?"

She pulled away from him.

"I am being serious. Leave him and come, be with me instead."

"Stop teasing me. Isn't it about time you put it to bed? Not literally of course. I mean your relationship with your own lady. If you are not that happy."

"Honestly, I'm not in love with Raquel. I can walk away. No problem there. But can you do the same? Leave him. Be with me. Please, seriously."

She moved forward and clasped her wet hands around his neck, "You make me feel amazing. So alive. This is so very wrong. You're a dangerous man, I think. You're very hard to resist, detective."

He nestled his head against her breasts, "Good. I just want to be with you. I feel the same being here, just with you. I'm sorry but pretending to be lost, that was the best way to be alone with you. I needed to test the water, so to speak."

She laughed heartily and it sounded so musical to his ears.

"But seriously, Phil. How do we do this? How do we let Steve, and his mother down? They will be hurt by our actions."

"Okay. Let's talk it over. It's nice here, so why rush back to camp? I think we tell your Steve as soon as we get back. We'll hurt him for sure, but it's better to tell him our feelings now, rather than we meet up behind his back. And I'll tell Raquel tonight, as soon as I see her."

"I imagine she'll be very upset."

"Yes, Kimberley. I imagine she will be. We've shared quite a bit in the past. I may have made a mistake by sharing too much with her. And this is exactly *what* it is. This feels real and it feels right to me. Please, believe me. I want be with you."

She shook her head, "I can't believe this. How fast it's all happened. Are you really sure?"

"I know my feelings are strong. Screw the rest of the world."

He clasped her soft right hand in his own, afraid to let go of her, in case he had imagined it all. The spell was only broken when they heard the distinct sound of footsteps crunching across ground cover. It sounded close by. They looked searchingly into each other's eyes, then looked down at their respective semi naked bodies. They raced back into the water hole, water splashing high around their thighs and placed a respectable distance between them.

Steve's head bobbed up at the top of the bank and he smiled down at them. He saw the pair of them were floating neck deep in the water hole. He had a strange, bewildered expression on his angular face.

"Hey, there you both are. Found you. I thought you two got lost in the bush. You know our camp site is just over the hill, about twenty metres away."

"Really? No. We must've gone around in complete circles," Duncan replied, placing his cock back into his pants. Fortunately for them, the water was dark and light reflective. Kimberley fiddled under the water surface too, frantically hooking the front of her sports bra together again.

"Yes, we were lost," Kimberley stated before she took a big gulp of air into her lungs and slipped under the water, in a bid to find her hastily discarded stretch jeans. She knew the removal of their t-shirts could be explained away, but her jeans might well betray them. She returned to the surface moments later, still without her jeans.

She pushed her wet hair back and gave Duncan a direct look of desperation.

He winked at her side on, so that his gesture was unseen by Steve and then confidently walked up the embankment. He did not care he was bare chested.

"We couldn't resist having a quick dip in the water hole," he said.

Steve Willaston sat down on the bank's edge and studied the pair of them. His expression was unreadable, but he appeared to be rattled, his eyebrows knitted together.

Kimberley took a big breath and dived again, to renew her desperate search for her jeans to cover up her modesty.

"I already saw you together. You do realise that your voices carried a bit on the wind. I heard some bits and pieces of what you said to my girlfriend."

Hearing Steve's words, Duncan froze in the water, which was now up to his naked waist.

Steve smirked as he glared at the detective's arrow straight back.

He stretched his body, hands on narrow hips and stepped closer to the water's edge. "So you're taking her away from me, are you? I can't believe you said it, to my girlfriend. You've completely lost my respect, if this is your plan. You will let her down too."

Duncan slightly moved his head and replied in his strong, firm tone, "Afraid you'll be proven wrong. Don't assume to know how I feel or what I will do."

Steve looked down at his feet, wiped a bead of water from the corner of his right eye which Duncan took for a solitary tear and sighed heavily, "I looked up to you. You were my reason to join the police force."

Kimberley bobbed up and took another deep breath and disappeared as the two men continued their exchange.

Duncan nodded his head and shrugged, "Unexpected things can happen. That's life."

"You're a bloody arsehole. You win, you get to keep her. I don't want to know what's next. But respect my mother.

You'd better do the right thing and tell her. Or I swear, I will tell her."

Steve turned his back but added through gritted teeth, "By the way, I'm leaving the camp now. You two can cosy up in your small crappy tent. I don't give a fuck."

****

Raquel walked briskly to the town's post office, to collect her daily mail. She was smartly dressed in a western check shirt and skinny jeans, a look which was a casual hangover from her heady Phil Proctor days. She was trying not to worry about Phil Duncan. He hadn't returned from the camping trip at the national park as yet, and his last text message said that he needed an extra day of 'fresh air and recreation.' Whatever that meant.

She dreaded collecting her mail. The post mistress used to deliver the mail around town on her old bicycle, but she toppled over the handlebars one day, trying to avoid an angry, swooping magpie. She broke her wrist and all of Brumby Flat elected to pick up their mail from the post office after that.

As usual, eighty-something Mavis Dexter was holding court inside, sorting through locals mail with her arthritic, grizzled hands at the front counter. She looked up over the top rims of her reading glasses and cracked a smile at Raquel when she entered.

She smiled back and could see that Mavis had forgotten her hearing aid again. She had also dyed her frizzy grey hair cobalt blue clearly by accident. She had a terrible time lately remembering to take her eyeglasses whenever she went shopping. But she was still sharp with figures and deciphering other people's mail.

"Hello, love," she croaked brightly and picked up a wad of envelopes to her left, "Here's your mail. I'm afraid there's not much here to be happy about."

Raquel nodded her head and outstretched her palm for the usual procedure. With Mavis around, keeping secrets of a postal nature were near impossible.

"Here's your water bill, by the look of it." Mavis said, popping the envelope on her palm, "Here's the rates notice and your electricity bill," she planted two more, "I thought you paid them last month. You don't want to get behind with these bills, my dear."

With a final flourish, she added two more to the pile, "I think this is a personal letter from your mother, and how is she, dear? And this must be your dentist bill. You've got such lovely teeth. Don't know what the dentist needed to do to them."

"Thanks, Mavis. Have to go."

"Oh wait. I forgot the last one. Your detective friend, well, he left this note here for you this morning. He dashed in and dashed out again. Seemed to be in a mad rush."

Mavis held the object aloft, in her right hand which was slightly shaking.

Raquel frowned, raised an eyebrow and gingerly took the private note from her which was thankfully concealed in a cheap envelope.

She turned on her heel and quickly glanced over the newspaper headlines as she did. One headline read, 'Park Murder Count link to Brumby Flat.' She shook her head and left the post office. She had planned to open his personal note back at the house. But she ripped it open right away and read it outside, shading her eyes from the glare of the sun with a cupped hand. The words were simple and painfully blunt in their instruction. It was written in his big scrawly handwriting. She had recognised it straight away.

"I have had a rethink of our current situation. Pack up. Move out of my house today."

She re-read his note several times over, trying to make sense of it. It took her a few minutes to realise that it was his way of breaking up with her. It shocked her, just how cruel it sounded. She found she didn't really want to challenge Duncan about it. She had no desire to call him to discuss the note. She was too angry and hurt to bother.

She walked briskly back to the house, with tears streaming freely down her cheeks. She wrestled with the front door and raced upstairs to the bedroom they had shared. She angrily started to toss her clothes from the oak wardrobe onto the bed in a heaped pile. Then she threw three pairs of her shoes on top of it. She opened a couple of bedside drawers and tipped everything out of them onto the bed they had shared together.

She galloped down the narrow stairs with the bundle of clothing in her arms. Dumping the pile on the ground, she fished her car keys out of her jeans back pocket and opened the drivers' door. She then threw the bundle into the back seat. She went upstairs again and did the same with the last armload of her personal gear.

She thought of leaving his front entrance door wide open, but then remembered she had her new dining room suite to pick up later. And she realised that she wasn't that much of a bitch. She stomped back to the house and locked the front door securely for him. She stopped in her tracks and fished out the shop keys from her jeans pocket. She opened the front door and threw them inside. She closed it again. She had no intention of keeping the Raindrops Shop open for Duncan ever again.

Then she remembered Maxine, the blue heeler she had inherited when Proctor had left the country. She opened the side gate and called her dog a couple of times. Finally, Maxine came striding up, tongue rolling over her jaw and wagging her tail enthusiastically.

"Come in, in the front. I hope you've peed all over the tennis court," Raquel opened the passenger door and Maxine quickly jumped up. She was strangely always happy to go for a drive, even if she had to stand indignant on the local vet's examination table.

"Well. Fuck him then," she said to herself through gritted teeth as she turned over the engine. She backed her Pontiac out of the driveway at speed, but fortunately no one else was around. She turned the steering wheel a hard left and disappeared down the street, leaving a dark plume of smoke behind her.

Chapter Seven

She had arrived at the Beecham's Bridge Thirty Second and a third Folk Festival clearing, flanked by towering gnarled old gumtrees, with her simple tent and meagre belongings packed haphazardly in her cumbersome, oversized backpack. She glanced around her surroundings, noting the raised stage with strings of paper lanterns and colourful fairy lights. She saw the hive of activity as stall holders were frantically setting up their tables of candles, handmade soaps, crafts and vegan treats, in preparation for the crowds who would start arriving when the festival gates opened later in the afternoon.

Misty Rae Phoenix was a fifty something aspiring folk singer. Over the years, she had moonlighted as a backing singer for a number of infamous indie bands, but she always came back to her roots. She preferred basking alone at markets and shopping malls.

She let the heavy backpack fall to the park's bark littered floor with a resounding thud. She stood there and stretched her arms and flexed her bare feet. Inhaling the eucalyptus-tinged air into her nostrils, she closed her squinty brown eyes in her tanned, weathered face. She was still beautiful in her own rugged way, her body lean and athletic for her age. She was carefully with what she ate, always drank litres of mineral water every day and practised her own unique version of yoga.

Her unruly long brown hair was braided in places, attached to an array of beads, feathers she had found and thin twisted strands of leather. Her hair was tied and smoothed into place with a colourful bandana. Her uniform of choice was usually a deep brown leather vest showing her belly button and trim midriff, teamed with her pleated floral skirt or colourful Bali trousers. Today, she had her favourite Bali trousers on. Misty Rae had finished her outfit with a string of mismatched beads and bracelets of jingling bells on her ankles. She found a position to the left of the first market stall and started to erect her small one-person tent. It didn't take her long because she was well practised in camping. When she had finished, she sat cross legged in front of the entrance of her tent. She picked up her battered guitar and started to sing for the stall holders. At least she had a captive audience for a change.

Her voice was a bit pitchy at times, but it was pleasant enough. It soared above the woodland chatter of birdsong. Her guitar playing was smooth and it was evident that she had learnt how to play at a young age. She came from a musical family. She learnt to play the guitar by ear and took piano lessons. Unfortunately, her identical twin sister Clare had exhibited no such talent. It had not been easy for her, being the odd one out. While the rest of the family, Misty Rae included, played a variety of musical instruments or sang in key at their gatherings, Clare would sit quietly in the corner, and whisper the words to songs. If she did choose to join in, the musical harmonies descended into an unfortunate musical melee.

Clare left home early and married a multi-millionaire. Misty Rae was strangely not heartbroken as she had felt no connection with Clare anyway. Unusual for identical twins. That's what people said.

Misty Rae launched into a bittersweet well-known love song for the stall holders who were starting to slow down their activity and just enjoy the natural surroundings and the free musical accompaniment. A few of them wandered over to her and threw money onto her handkerchief on the ground and smiled. Misty Rae was grateful as the extra money would fund her nomad lifestyle, and hopefully propel her to a music festival in another state.

It was a hard life with limited reward, but the money she earned from busking was enough for her to get by. She made enough money to be free, live her nomadic existence with her few possessions and her treasured bespoke guitar, made by a family friend. She told herself that it was enough for her to get by.

She stopped her performance after a softer ballad. A few stall holders clapped her as she pulled the guitar strap up over her head.

She saw a figure come forward, still clapping his hands loudly together.

"Cool stuff. You're really bloody good."

She smiled, "Thank you."

Raquel Willaston's former long-time lover Ricardo stood there, smirking. He was dressed in his security uniform, looking much the same as he did two years earlier when he was in Brumby Flat during the time of the infamous murders. He had just a touch more salt than pepper in his hair and his paunch was a bit more noticeable. He had called Raquel of course, hoping to catch up with her in nearby Brumby Flat but she had made a mention that she was sorting out a relationship issue.

He had just watched Misty Rae's performance, liked her look and decided to take a chance to approach her, "Hey, I'm Ricardo. Call me Rick for short."

"Nice to meet you, Rick."

"If you need a security escort, I'm your man," he said with a sly wink, keeping pace next to her.

"I'm right, but thank you," she reached for his hand and pointed to his wedding band.

He shrugged his shoulders, "If you need anything, just ask me."

"Okay, I will."

She gave him an awkward, small wave and headed down the dirt trail, towards the Batty Roadhouse.

****

Hazel Willaston elegantly climbed out of her company car, smoothing her tight pencil skirt discreetly into place and slammed the door firmly shut. She teetered on her high heels and smoothed her grey hair into place which was tied back in a polished bun updo. She had been forced to leave an important corporate meeting to learn what was going on with her daughter and her policeman grandson. She had sent both of them text messages and made a series of unanswered calls for days. Finally, frustrated by the sounds of silence, she made the long drive up to Brumby Flat. It was a risky move as she was the CEO of a pet food company which was going through a radical corporate board reshuffle. There were a couple of senior members literally snapping at her heels, vying for her enviable position.

She found the key to Raquel's house in the bottom of her laptop bag and fiddled with the latch until the front door swung wide open. She entered and recoiled immediately at the smell of dust and neglect which suffocated her nostrils. She knew her daughter had an aversion to housework.

"Hello, coo-eee! Is anyone home?" She had a small girl's voice, but she yelled out through the hallway with no difficulty, her red stiletto heels echoing across the timber floor. Fortunately, she was small in stature, and the indents left behind were barely visible.

She had to negotiate her way around towering piles of unopened boxes, trying to take great care not to get dust and cobwebs over her brand new, immaculate black houndstooth patterned suit. Fortunately, she was skinny enough to get past without any mishap.

Raquel emerged from the depths of her darkened bedroom, cradling her dark circled eyes from the sun glare and wrapping her bathrobe consciously over her underwear when she saw who it was.

"Oh, it's just you, mother. I thought someone was actually being murdered in my own home," she remarked. She rubbed her hazel eyes and started to cry again. The tears made slimy black trails of mascara mark her cheeks.

"Good god, what's wrong with you? Where's my grandson, Steve? I haven't been able to get any of you on the phone for days. I was getting so worried."

Steve had heard all the commotion, and he also walked out of his corner of the house, rubbing his red tinged eyes.

"Nan, how are you doing?" He said, in a miserable tone of voice. He was dressed head to toe in black which suited his gloomy mood.

Raquel's mother winced and waved her hands around.

"Really? You're upset too? What's going on with you two?" She demanded, turning on a spiky heel and heading to the kitchen which she found full of dirty dishes piled high in the sink, "Look at this mess," she said, ending the sentence with an aspirated sigh.

"Well, I guess you'd better know. Detective Phillip Duncan left me. It was brutal how he did it too," Raquel started to softly sob again on the sleeve of her bathrobe.

Steve added, "Yeah, he broke up with Raquel and my girlfriend left me for him," he started to cry, and no one could understand the rest of his words. Tears streamed down his cheeks and his words were lost in a series of hiccups which followed. He then retreated to his corner of the house.

Raquel continued to explain, "Detective Duncan ran off with his girlfriend Kimberley, that's what he's trying to say."

Her mother frowned and carefully flicked on the kettle on the bench with a manicured forefinger.

"I knew it. I did warn you about that man, didn't I? He looked like a shifty, spineless character to me. I don't understand why you left the cowboy, Raquel. He was such a nice tall gentleman. I'm pretty sure he adored you."

Raquel patted down her unruly unwashed hair and said through gritted teeth.

"No. *He* left me, mother."

"No doubt you said something wrong which upset him. You did that to your father on a number of occasions too. I was always the level-headed one in the middle of all your nonsense. Here. Let's have a coffee together. You can tell me all about it."

"Mother, I don't want to talk about it. And Steve's upset. He was really besotted with his girlfriend, Kimberley."

Hazel shook her head and flicked her gaze to the kitchen ceiling which was full of cobwebs. She studied it for a moment, then gave up thinking about it.

"Oh god. He's still very young, he'll soon get over it. Another girl will come along and he'll forget the hurt. But you, on the other hand, you've wasted years of your life on a string of no-good men. They are forever leaving you, aren't they, dear?"

Raquel flopped herself onto one of her stools and cradled her head, readying herself for another barrage of her mother's thoughts on her life choices. But it didn't come. Hazel said nothing more, just continued to make instant coffee for them both.

"Well then, how's your corporate life going?" She asked, making small talk.

Her mother snorted, "Thanks for asking. It's a bit shit just at the moment, dear. I'm fending off attacks from all sides by interested stakeholders in Ripper Eats and Treats. But I survived the last merger, so I know I can survive this one too. Not a biggie to a veteran player, such as myself."

"And how is your latest toyboy? Is he well?"

Hazel screwed up her nose and lunged for the kettle which had just finished boiling, "I don't understand your intense interest in my love life. Toyboys have their short term uses, if you must know. It's not a long-lasting thing. Just a pleasing thing."

She splashed the boiling hot water into unmatched mugs. She followed it with a liberal splash of long-life skim milk into each one.

"I look, but I don't actually touch. That's where we differ."

"So I've noticed. And you seem to fall for men more like your father. But I did like your cowboy. He had this sexual chemistry about him. I was very attracted to your man, and I'm not afraid to tell you."

Raquel shook her head and reached for the proffered coffee mug, "Thanks for the honesty. Just what a daughter wants to hear from her own adoring mother."

"That's fine, dear. My advice to you costs you nothing. Now. Steve needs to build his bridge and get over it. I think that's the expression. In your case, it's more like you need to get back on that horse and ride it. *That* works well for me, since I left your father."

Chapter Eight

Janine Peterson yawned and stretched her chubby forearms out, then swivelled her creaky office chair right around to look at her husband. Her facial features were exactly replicated in her daughter Banksia. She carefully removed her reading glasses which were caught up in her naturally curly, greying hair and reflectively said, "I can't believe you did it. You actually stepped outside our house today."

Bob Peterson shrugged his round shoulders and rubbed his bulbous nose on the neckline of his rock band t-shirt, "Yes, I did. It felt surreal. Been a long time but I got some amazing photography in my camera. I'll unload it on the computer later so you can view it all."

She returned to look at her illuminated computer screen. She was halfway through reading a scientific journal online which was holding her interest, "Looking forward to it. But did you find or see anything interesting out there? That's what I really would like to know."

He slouched in his chair which creaked under his weight, as he reached for the bowl of potato chips their daughter had left them, "Yes, I did. Lots of birds, parrots mainly. I saw a wombat and then I came across an old van hidden deep in the scrub. It looked like someone had set fire to it, but I think it must've happened ages ago."

"A van?"

"It looked like an old kombi van. And before I stumbled on it, I bumped into a couple of locals on the trail. I said hello to them, but I kept on walking. They looked a bit ratty to me."

"Fair enough. Should we be telling anyone about the kombi van?"

He shrugged his shoulders, "Probably. I'll send an email straight after dinner. Only trouble is, it may bring strangers here. I like our busy solitude."

His wife nodded her head and kept reading. Bob stared at his own screen, stuffing a handful of potato chips into his mouth. Since their daughter had taken over the running of the Batty Roadhouse, they spent their time working on their academic papers, eating junk food and retreating further away from all human connection. They had lost touch with their old friends but had grown closer together as a married couple.

Suddenly, Janine twisted her squeaky swivel chair towards the door.

"Did you hear that?" She said in a low whisper, "What's that sound?'

Bob twisted his lips, furrowed his bushy eyebrows and narrowed his eyes. He dusted his potato chip hands across the front of his t-shirt.

"Sounds like someone's knocking on our front door."

"Can't be our Banksia. What do we do?"

"We let them in, I guess that's what we do."

"Okay. Tell whoever it is to come around the back, to the kitchen door. You can handle it, dear."

Bob got up and pulled his t-shirt down over his bare round belly, "Don't stress. I'll go to the front door and open it. Sooner or later, we need to let the world in."

He disappeared into the dark hallway, his weighty footsteps echoing across the timber floorboards. She heard the front door creak open on its hinges, excited raised voices, the shuffle of feet and then nothing.

She readjusted her glasses and cried out, in an uncertain tone, "Bob. Are you okay? Who was it at our door?"

There was no answer.

She cried out his name again, feeling a sense of anxiety. What was he doing? He was taking a bit of time dealing with whoever it was at the front door.

"BOB!"

The barrel of a gun clearly appeared out from the shadows, and it was the last image Janine Peterson would ever see. It went off, opening a gaping bloody cavity in her chest.

****

Hannah Dee Wainwright climbed out of her close to, but not quite yet vintage car. She removed her oversized reflective aviator sunglasses and frowned at the sight of the tired looking Batty Roadhouse. Her smoky eyeliner had smudged in the wind. She heaved a big sigh and drummed her fingers on the open door of her bright pink convertible. She only lifted her fingers to slap a large mozzie which had hovered and then landed safely on her neck undetected. It left her with a nice, raised red bump. She slapped it dead just one second too late.

"Well, Fuck. That's just bloody great," she said aloud to no one in particular, only to herself. She removed a partially squashed cigarette out of her designer handbag and lit it with a cheap flick lighter. She took a long drag and exhaled a puff of smoke. She had eagerly signed up to be the headline act with her backing band at the thirty-second and a third Beecham's Bridge Folk Festival and had high expectations for her accommodation. Now, after seeing the roadhouse in the dying last glimmer of daylight, she realised her hotel room may not be quite up to scratch. She shook her mane of wavy blonde hair and fluffed up the faux fur trim of her moderately expensive white parka. Holding the cigarette poised high in her right hand, she began her confident walk towards the building, her designer black ankle boots making loud scrunching sounds across the gravel drive.

The automatic glass doors opened, and she entered to confront Banksia who was humming softly to herself and dusting the shelves in front of the shop counter.

"I am here," Hannah announced to all, a hand resting on a hip, as she took another contented long puff on her cigarette and stepped inside.

Banksia stopped her shelf dusting and glared back at the stranger. Roadhouse regulars' old Chook and neighbouring farmer Barb Hillman who sat plonked on their favourite stools, glanced up from their plates of homemade pies splashed with generous blobs of tomato sauce. Barb then calmly turned her back on the intruder and completed her personal story to Chook. "Yeah, mate. It really happened. He said exactly that to the little shithead. I'm not bullshitin' you around."

"Hey. I don't care *who* you are, but you can't smoke in here," Banksia snapped at the stranger, looking her up and down.

"Fine," Hannah tossed her cigarette down onto the tiled floor and squashed it angrily under the heel of her right boot, leaving a smudged patch of blackened ash.

"Now. As I *said* I have arrived. Where's my bloody hotel room? I want to freshen up immediately."

Old Chook coughed while Barb giggled into her coffee mug and they exchanged knowing looks between themselves.

"Hotel?" Banksia tossed her head and smirked, "Sorry. This isn't a hotel. I do have three motel rooms at the back. Ah, right. Are you part of the festival entertainment?"

"My band and I, we *are* the headline act. Everyone is coming here to see me and the boys perform."

"Okay. Well then. Is it Hannah? I've prepared your room."

"Good. Terrific. And?"

"This way. Sorry, guys, I'll be back soon," Banksia headed towards the kitchen and picked up a hand towel and a cake of soap from the side cabinet. As they walked through the old swing back door, she turned slightly and threw the items directly to her guest.

Hannah just managed to catch them in time, clutching the towel tight against her chest. She was not impressed but said nothing. She continued to follow the young woman. As she walked over the rough, uneven ground she waved a few blowflies away from her face.

"Wow, your flies are real bad here," she remarked.

Banksia said nothing. She continued to stomp step her way over the dry groundcover.

The motel building came into sight which made her stop completely in her tracks. It was just a large transportable building with three separate doors which opened onto a wide timber deck veranda. Banksia climbed up the couple of steps and fiddled with the key in the lock of the first door.

"There you go. Your room," she said with a touch of sarcasm and swung the door wide open.

Hannah stepped inside, and noted the dark timber lined walls and the smoke-stained ceiling, along with a strong musty smell hanging in the stale air. There was a narrow table with a small television and a double bed with an abstract patterned bedspread which had seen much better days. On top of the bed, there was a couple of extra white towels. A flimsy wicker chair crisscrossed with cobwebs sat neglected in the corner. She went further inside and found a door leading into a toilet.

"So, where's the fuckin' bathroom?"

Banksia half smiled and replied, "There's no bathroom in any of these units. There is a small hand basin in the toilet but if you need to shower, you can't. But there is a large claw foot bath out back. I reclaimed it from a farmers' paddock, just for you. It's between the water tank and a timber wall. You pull over the shower curtain for privacy."

"Really? How does that work?"

"Simple. I'm really glad you asked me. You can swing the pole with the curtain over the entrance, so people know it's being used. There's a water hose nearby. You turn the tap on. You then fill the bath and you use it. It's best to have your bath when the sun's out. The water's icy cold."

Hannah shook her head and pushed her parker back as she placed her hands on her hips defiantly, "You're nuts. I can't have a cold bath out in public. I'm contacting my agent about this."

"Okay. Leave it with you. I've got other customers to attend to. If you need me, you know where to find me," Banksia retreated from the room and quietly shut the door behind her.

Hannah whipped out her mobile phone and pressed her thumb hard on the contact she needed to talk to, "Des. It's me, Hannah. What fuckin' shithole did you book for me at the Folk Festival? It's not a hotel. It's like a nightmare I've woken up in. It's a fuckin' joke."

Tour promoter Des Rundall was hosting a female guest in his massive eight-person spa when his second-best star called him. He put her on loudspeaker, as he relaxed with the soapy spa bubbles bursting all around him. He wasn't an attractive man but his position within the music industry gave him an aura of sexual competence. He had a pronounced bald spot on the top of his head and two bushy caterpillar eyebrows over a pair of deep brown shrewd, but squinty eyes. He sipped away at his whisky glass, playing a calculated game of toesies with the cute, topless brunette opposite him in the spa.

"Now, now. Slow down, Hannah. Tell me what's happening. What's the matter, my sweet baby girl? You know how important you are to me. You're my girl with the golden vocals."

"Des. You need to find me some place elsewhere to stay. I'm in some run-down old shack at the back of an ugly roadhouse."

"My lovely, there's not a lot of options going where you are. You're smack bang in the middle of nowhere, in case you haven't noticed," he laughed, winking at his young twenty-something companion who smiled sweetly back. She then arched her back and shifted slightly forward, her feet reaching for his private parts. She teased him further by licking her ruby red lips just above the bubbles.

Des felt his dick shoot up in a hard salute. He lowered his voice and said, "Hannah, my love, this is the best place for you. I know you well. You don't want to drive fifty kilometres away to make it to your big gig coming up. From some place called something Flat something. Anyway, you're right there, at the national park and it's just a short ten-minute walk to the stage. How magical is that?"

"But Des…" she tried to protest.

He immediately rebutted her, "My darling, Hannah, that's quite enough. Try and make the best of the situation. Try to make it work for you. It's just the way that it has to be."

Hannah flicked her pale grey eyes to the discoloured ceiling above her, "Okay. But I am the headline act."

"I know. I know. You are Hannah Dee Wainwright. The caster of many magical and musical spells. And anyway, you and the lads are only staying over a couple of nights, well, three nights. Surely you can put up with just a little inconvenience."

"Des. The bathroom is not even a real bathroom. It's just an old grubby bathtub plonked in their back yard. I'm the star and I will be exposed to all the elements," she snorted.

Des laughed heartily, winking at his companion again. She had moved closer to him now, her full breasts bouncing on the surface of the warm bubbling water. He leaned forward and cupped his hands underneath their softness and squeezed them together.

"Well, okay. That is befitting a forest nymph like yourself, Lovey. Just take it in your stride and show them all what you got. You're my beautiful big star. Let your goddamn talent shine."

"Oh, Des." She could feel her cheeks blushing pink.

"It's true. Now, I have to go. I have some rather pressing matters to attend to. Good luck with the thirty-second and a third Anniversary Folk Festival in that crazy wild park. They're saying that ticket sales have hit triple figures already. Good job, Hannah."

Hannah closed the call and cast her eyes around her drab motel room again. She found the wall mirror next to the television and studied her reflection in it carefully. She had been a sort of 'star' for the last ten years, and when she had begun, she looked barely twenty rather than twenty-five which she really was. She had just turned thirty-six recently and she was trying hard to pretend she could still roll and run with the twenty-somethings. However, she could see the dark circles under her eyes from too many boozy late nights. Fine crow's feet lines had suddenly appeared at the corners of her eyes. A couple of grey hairs had also popped up overnight which she quickly plucked out. In future, she knew she would have to dye her hair more frequently. She also knew she shouldn't chain smoke, but the pressures of being the second-best entertainment act on her promoters' books, increased her anxiety level. At least she wasn't the third best but she felt she deserved to be the best paid.

Hannah lived only to perform on a stage. Her raspy, raw edged voice perfectly suited the folk songs her band could play. Unfortunately, she didn't want to pay top dollar for her backing band, so they were very average musicians at best. Every now and again, they got lost and there was often an empty gap she had to fill with her searing voice and some impromptu drawn-out vocal gymnastics. Sometimes, she just came to a screeching halt when the music trailed off and talked to the audience. She had become quite good at covering up all their bung notes, lack of melodic cohesion and their over reliance on the G note.

She flicked her wavy blonde hair to one side and reapplied her mascara as she puffed away on the fresh cigarette she had popped between her frosty pink full lips. Her mobile started to ring.

She re-dipped her mascara brush, bent over in front of the small wall mirror and exhaled a steady stream of smoke as she answered.

"Hey, Brody mate, where in hell are you guys?"

"We're nearly there. I think we're about five minutes away. Are we having a rehearsal tonight?"

She gave it a long thought, knowing full well they needed to run through the playlist, but she dismissed it, "First thing in the morning, when we're doing the sound check. I'm tired anyway. See you in the morning. By the way, you're not going to like the accommodation. It's like bug city here. Drop by my room, Brody. Okay?"

She then walked into the toilet and moments later, she let out a bloodcurdling scream.

****

Banksia had returned to the kitchen and had begun prepping a chicken burger for the early evening takeaway food rush. Old Chook was griping about the folk festival to Barb Hillman who was leaning in and always patient with him. He told her it may bring undesirable elements to the farming district. Banksia was half listening to their conversation.

The phone on the wall suddenly started to ring as she flipped the burger on the griller.

"Hello? Batty Roadhouse," She replied wistfully. She listened to the angry female voice on the other end.

"A big bloody spider in the toilet?" She repeated, "No, I don't have to come to your room. I left you a can of insect spray in the cabinet next to the television…Yep, thanks. Do that."

Detective Duncan strode in as Banksia hung up the phone very firmly. He nodded his acknowledgment to the locals who were busy talking about personal matters.

"Is there trouble?" He asked Banksia in his strong, commanding tone. He adjusted his glasses on the bridge of his nose. He was wearing his best tan trousers with a black rolled neck skivvy which clung to his well-toned chest.

She shook her head and waved a dismissive hand, "Naw. All good, detective. Nothing I can't handle."

She returned to the kitchen in time to flip the burger over again.

"Were you after a meal?" She yelled out to him.

"Yeah. I'm happy with a burger if you're making one."

Suddenly, the phone started to ring again. She put aside the greasy turner and wiped her hands across her apron to answer it.

"Yes, Batty Roadhouse."

Duncan sat down on the same wonky stool and dropped an inch, watching her as she listened to the caller and flicked her eyes to the ceiling and shrugged her shoulders in his direction.

He made a mental note of all her too obvious signals of aspiration.

"So, you reckon the largest cockroach in the known universe went running under your bed? Right. Use the bug spray again. Maybe spray your whole room with it…Yep. Okay. You do that."

She hung up and frowned at the phone.

"She'd better not call me all bloody night. For Christ's sake."

"Who was that?"

"Oh, it's that crazy hippie diva star in room one. In my motel. You'd think they don't get flies, spiders and cockroaches in the city, seriously."

Duncan smirked, "She sounds a bit too delicate for the country lifestyle."

"You're not wrong. I bloody hope she has talent, not just a loud unpleasant manner. What are you doing here anyway?"

"I'm staying over for the duration of the Folk Festival. Hope you don't mind but I've parked my caravan on the side. It's sort of more around the back."

"You know," she said as she took the burger and pan off the burner, "You don't strike me as a music festival type."

"Well okay. This is just between you and me. I'm going to do my best to blend in. But I am here to observe the festival and do some serious people watching."

She knitted her eyebrows together as she finished the hamburger with a flourish of mayonnaise, some lettuce and an overripe slice of tomato. She studied him under her new fringe cut which covered her high forehead perfectly.

"You don't think anything bad is going to happen during the festival, do you?" She asked.

He shrugged his shoulders, "Hopefully not. If you notice anything suspicious at all, call me at once, okay?"

Barb Hillman suddenly leaned over Duncan's left shoulder, her tanned right hand squeezing it, and he didn't particularly like her invasion of his personal space. She smelled strongly of cigarette smoke, dust and horse manure. He leaned a good inch away. But she was not the type to take a hint either.

Barb had no filter and merely smiled at him, showing the wide gap in her top front teeth.

"Hey, I heard you two discussing the pretty singer. I'll have to lift my game I guess. Banks, I will need to buy some lippy off you," she chortled.

"Yeah, sure thing. I have a fuchsia pink shade or something called burnt orange. I have a rouge too if you need it. Over there, on the top shelf."

"Thanks, love. Well. On my own now. Chook's gone and cracked the shits on me and he up and left. What do you do?"

****

The next morning as the first shards of sunlight infiltrated the motel room, Hannah stretched her arms up and out and sat up on the bed, the sheet tucked under her chin. She turned her head just enough to see Brody still lying sound asleep on his left side. He doubled as the lead guitarist for her backing band and he served as her squeezable toy boy whenever she had a crisis which happened to be quite often.

During her first night in the Batty motel, he had saved her from a number of spiders, sized from large to tiny and various insects which were found to be sharing her room. As a reward, she gave him a blowjob and let him cosy up to her and stay the night. He was happy not to shack up with his boozy band mates in the adjoining room.

She rose from the creaky double bed naked, her pert pale breasts jiggling as she reached for her slip floral dress draped over the wicker chair in the room. She slipped it over her head and adjusted it in place over her body. Part of her morning routine, she also reached for her packet of ciggies on the table. She yawned loudly, and had lit a cigarette before she opened the front door to greet the day. Sunlight was gently streaming across the timber veranda through the lattice framework in jagged, intricate patterns. She walked on her bare feet to the edge of the veranda and leaned against the timber railings. With her free right hand, she fanned her blonde hair out and then cupped it over her pale grey eyes, to shade them from the sun's fierce glare.

As she stood there, smoking away, she admired the surrounding bushland. She had to admit that the national park was a green haven at the early flourish of spring. It would be an amazing backdrop for her performance. They would be sharing the stage with five other acts over the weekend, which did not share her longevity as a performer. At least she had released two studio albums and had an agent to back her.

Hannah saw movement to the left and glanced momentarily in that direction. Detective Duncan jogged past, right under her nose. She admired his tall, strong, lithe physicality. She idly thought that he moved like a black panther with fluid, reserved movements.

He only turned around mid-pace when he heard her belt out a high-pitched scream.

She was perched up high in the corner of the veranda, eyes wide as she stared down a small kangaroo which had hopped onto the timber decking to join her.

"Are you okay?" He asked her, in a perfectly clear voice, unaffected by his vigorous run through the national park. His hands rested on his hips, his black lycra pants hugging all his taunt leg muscles. The kangaroo turned it's angular head and hopped away, back into the bushes it had sprung from.

Hannah quickly composed herself and retrieved the cigarette that she had dropped in fright. She shook her hair out and coyly smiled back.

"Hello. Yes, thanks, I'm fine. That 'roo bloody scared the living crap out of me," she said, trying hard to flirt.

Duncan smirked and stepped closer, "If you're not used to them, but they are pretty much everywhere up here. Won't hurt you."

"It's a wild animal."

Suddenly, the front door of her motel room burst wide open and young Brody stood there with only a white towel wrapped over his slim hips. His brown hair was ruffled from last nights' fight with the pillow and some pretty wild sex with her.

"Hey. Is everything all right? Heard you scream," he stood there, scratching his bare belly and yawning.

Hannah sucked hard on her ciggie and screwed up her face as she exhaled the smoke.

Her chances of striking up a cosy conversation with the mysterious, fit stranger had evaporated like the proverbial puff of smoke she blew out.

Duncan nodded his head and looked down at his feet and runners, "Well, I'd say you don't require my services. Enjoy your day."

He turned away and as he jogged off, she leaned against the railing and watched his round buttocks disappear down the dirt track.

Brody nudged her with an elbow, "Who's your mate?" He asked.

"Nobody I will ever know…apparently."

She squashed out the cigarette on the top railing and then tried to rub away its black stain. She regretted her action for a fleeting moment.

"Brody, you'd better go back to your room now. Tell the guys there's a rehearsal in two hours. We need to nail my new song for this concert."

He smiled and scratched his lean belly, "Or else we get the sack?"

"Pretty much."

Chapter Nine

Hannah had finished her private tour of the concert perimeters, having made both the stage manager and her private secretary break down into unintelligible bundles of frustration and mess soon afterwards.

She now stood confidently on the stage platform in the centre of a clearing. Around the edges of bushland, market stalls were in various stages of frenetic set up.

Surrounded by huge gumtrees and the sounds of humanity conforming the space to suit its purpose, Hannah gripped the microphone tight in her hands and shut her pale grey eyes which were edged with a smear of gold glitter and blue eyeliner. She had changed out of the floral slip dress and being the diva she was, she had changed into a vintage orange shift mini dress with her sheer dark green cape over it, another fortunate op shop find. She was wearing her favourite piece of jewellery, a black plastic peace symbol on a long silver chain. She waited impatiently for the band to catch up with her. Once again, they had failed to keep up the pace and got lost in their notes. Brody, the lead guitarist was the better player of the band trio, but once the drummer lost the beat, he had crashed too.

Hannah was frustrated with all of them this morning. She drummed her fingers impatiently on the microphone and flicked her hair off her face, and said with a terse voice, "Guys, guys. You're killing it. But in the wrong bloody way. We play this fuckin' song in every set. Every gig we do. It's my biggest fuckin' hit. How can you stuff it up? Yet again? Tell me how you manage it?"

"Because you pay us shit wages," Greg snarled from behind his drum set and issued a brief solo with a flourish, "if you paid us some more money, maybe we'd be motivated to practice."

Hannah frowned which only emphasised the fine lines around her eyes and confirmed she was older than the boys.

"That's not fair. Look where we are now. We are headlining a major music festival tonight. Should be grateful that I managed to pull this one off. So, pull your fuckin' head in and concentrate on this shit."

Greg smashed his drumsticks down on the cymbals and replied with a liberal dose of sarcasm, "Yes, boss."

She tossed her hair back and rattled off another countdown, "On one…two…one, two, three…" She started to belt out her signature song, her one big radio hit, which had reached number forty-five on the Australian music charts. After a minute into the song, Greg had completely lost his place and Davo had stuck a bum note on his organ.

Hannah stopped halfway through the chorus and let the mic fall onto the spongey particleboard floor with a booming thud.

"That's it. Guys, guys. Just stop. You're just wasting my fuckin' time. You can't play for shit, Greg," she hissed at him. He smirked back and only shrugged his shoulders.

She then turned her attention to the sound guy, also named Greg, who had copped her diva-ish behaviour earlier.

"Hey, sound guy. Greg two. Can you turn me up and turn them down? Thank you very much."

He inclined his head, adjusting a few knobs on the consol.

"Okay. Let's try again. On three. One, two, three…"

Davo and Brody made a brief flourish of noise together, but her drummer just sat there, his drumsticks raised in the air. Hannah got five notes out, stopped and frowned. She popped the mic back into its stand with an angry flourish.

"Fine. Fuck it, Greg. I'm outta here. Going back to my room," she snapped at them. She stomped off the stage, her gossamer cape billowing behind her, as she negotiated the series of steps off stage in her knee-high boots.

"Hannah. I don't think he meant what he said. It's just the drink talking," Brody chased her down the side steps to ground level, propping his guitar over his shoulder.

As her boots touched the dirt, Misty Rae appeared practically out of nowhere. She stood in front of Hannah, twisting one of her hair braids and gripping her guitar strap with her other hand. She was still in her leather vest and her Bali trousers.

"Hey Hannah Dee," she chirped excitedly, hopping around her idol who was trying to goose step her way around her, "Nice to bump into you like this. I really admire you."

"That's nice."

"You must be looking forward to the festival tonight."

"Yeah, definitely. And who are you?"

"Me? Oh wow. I am, like, a nobody, just trying to be a somebody. I'm Misty Rae."

She put out her tanned hand out to shake hers, but Hannah dramatically pulled away.

"Well, Misty Rae. If you're after my autograph, you can fuckin' line up with the rest of the crowds, *after* my concert. Now, fuck off."

Misty Rae stopped in her tracks and stood still in the middle of the clearing, her mouth wide open in shock. She watched Hannah disappear down the trail to the roadhouse, with young Brody in hot pursuit.

"Well. Fuck you too, lady," she said aloud, lifting her middle finger high in the air and then, headed back towards her tent.

As Hannah walked on, she turned her head and walked a few steps backward, studying Brody's youthful face, "Look, don't keep covering for Greg all the time. He's an idiot kid who thinks he knows everything. Well, he has no fuckin' idea how the music industry really works. But luckily, I do. It was hard to score this gig for us. I had to really talk up you guys with Des. We nearly lost the gig to Cleo and her band. Of all people. But I managed to turn it around for us."

Brody nodded, "Yeah, I know. We all appreciate it. Especially me."

Hannah flicked her eyes up to the sky and continued walking down the dirt trail. Her knee-high cream boots were not built to cover the uneven ground, but she tried her best to keep perched on them. For the most part, she managed to keep her balance. Whenever she did stumble, Brody rushed forward and immediately grabbed her arm to steady her. She would smack his hand away angrily.

They arrived at the makeshift barrier fencing, where a security guard, as wide as he was tall bailed them up.

"Passes," he snapped.

"Crap. This too I have to deal with," Hannah felt under her dress collar and dragged out her stage pass lanyard for him to gawk at. "You should know who the fuck I am. Everyone knows me. My picture's on the bloody poster."

He nodded, letting her and Brody walk through.

They walked in silence for a couple of minutes, before Hannah continued her rant.

"I don't understand Greg's attitude. It's like he doesn't want to achieve anything in his life, nothing of any value," she snapped.

"It's not like that. He wasn't thinking clearly this morning at sound check. The drink was talking."

"Well, he's got one more chance with me. That's it. I am over his bad attitude."

They headed down the meandering dirt path. She had decided to have a bath after all, and freshen up before the concert. She turned her head every now and then, and looked around nervously.

She kept hearing sounds from the bushes as they walked along the trail.

"There? Brody. Did you hear that?" She stopped walking and tugged at Brody's shirt sleeve.

"What? No. I don't hear anything,"

"I think someone's following us."

"No. We're in the middle of the bush, Hannah. Probably 'roos and other bush animals around. Nothing to worry about."

"I don't know about that. I really do feel like we're being watched."

He shrugged off her fears and grinned broadly, "I don't think so. Just nature."

"Nature? I've got a petri dish of microorganisms just in my room."

She started walking forward again and turned her head back one more time. She was certain that an unseen pair of eyes were watching them closely.

They finally arrived back at the motel building and went to their respective rooms. Brody said that he was going to lie down and sleep for a couple of hours.

Hannah peered down at the cheap ten-dollar wristwatch she wore. Most of her earnings went on designer shoes and sunglasses which were on show whenever she appeared on stage, so she knew she could get away with wearing a cheap watch. She calculated that she had about seven hours until showtime. She carefully peeled off her sheer cape and stooped over to study her pale complexion in the small mirror.

She made a quick phone call to the roadhouse, putting in an order for lunch.

"Yes, that's right. Lunch to my room…I hope I don't have to keep repeating myself. Please bring me a warm strong lemon tea and a steak sandwich. Now, the steak has to be medium, no tomatoes, but onions are okay. Just a smudge of barbeque sauce on top. No salt but a dash of pepper…Yes. To my room in about fifty minutes…Maybe make it an hour. And incidentally, for your future reference, I've written down a list of what foods I can eat and what I can't…yeah, your breakfast was just okay. The eggs were too runny, and the bacon was tough. I expect a better result by tomorrow, okay…thanks very much."

She piled her hair up in a high ponytail and secured it with a rubber band into a twisted bun. She headed to the makeshift bathroom which Banksia had set up for her exclusively, with cake of soap and towels in hand. She wasn't looking forward to the experience.

She stopped dead in her tracks, juggled with the towels as she checked her side pocket for her packet of ciggies. She cursed when she realised she had left them back at her room and thought about turning around. But she decided to plod on and smoke two ciggies when she got back.

She found her private bathing space with ease. It was exactly where it was, as described by Banksia. It was hidden by a psychedelic patterned, colourful shower curtain propped up by a broom handle slung across the old rusty water tank and shoved into a lattice timber screen covered in ivy on the other end.

She gingerly lifted the garish shower curtain and ducked inside. Things did not get much better from there. She was faced with an old pink enamel bathtub with claw feet and a garden tap with half a hose attached. She carefully placed the towels and soap on the protruding cement base of the rusty old water tank.

She stood there, hands on hips, staring in dismay at her bespoke bathroom in the centre of the park, under the cloudless blue sky of day.

"Fuck me."

She bent down and picked up a hair dryer lying on the ground. She turned it over and looked at it more closely. It looked to be brand new. She was even more surprised to find a long electrical cord attached to it which disappeared under the door of the tool shed adjacent. She pressed the 'on' button and the hair dryer blew hot on her right palm. She switched it off and placed it back on the patch of grass. At least Banksia had got one thing right for her.

Hannah pulled the shower curtain tight across the pole to ensure there were no visible gaps. She then tossed the hose into the bath and turned the water tap on full. She let the bath fill up and sang to herself as she waited. Twenty minutes later, she turned the tap off and dipped her hand into the water. It felt ice cold, but she knew once she hopped in, she'd warm up quick smart. The sun was sitting high in the pale blue sky and fortunately it was a warmer than usual spring day.

She eagerly removed her vintage mini dress over her head and took off her black lace bra. She decided to leave just her cotton undies on. She climbed into the bath, holding the cake of soap and stood there for a good minute, shivering and shrieking, her arms wrapped over her breasts. Her nipples jutted out, provoked by the icy cold water. She gradually sunk deeper and deeper into the cold water, until it was lapping around the generous curves of her creamy breasts.

After five minutes, she was able to ease her back against the curve of the bath and she started rubbing the foaming soap over her lithe arms. A small, agile honeyeater flitted its way around the water tank area.

She was humming quietly to herself, smiling at the little bird and smoothing the soap over her long, pale throat. She was beginning to quite enjoy her open-air bathing experience, more than she had imagined she would. In fact, she even let her blonde ponytail unravel and tossed the rubber band away. She closed her pale grey eyes and dunked her head back into the bath water. Her blonde hair spread over the surface like an intricate spiders' web. When she resurfaced, she had to refocus her eyes and wipe the soap suds away from them. There was still a touch of gold glitter dancing on her eyelids.

Something had changed in her immediate surroundings. She sensed the change, rather than actually saw what it was. The pleasant background of birdsong had turned into a series of frenetic warning whistles. The small honeyeater had taken flight and disappeared. She saw a kookaburra take wing from a nearby gumtree. She clutched the edges of the bath and leaned forward, frowning.

Suddenly, a large shape flashed past on her left and she saw an object arc towards her, slicing the air. It landed with a splash in front of her and her whole body shook and vibrated intensely. She fell back, her head flopping against the back of the bathtub, her eyes wide and listless. Her face gently slipped under the surface of the bath water a few moments later. Just like that, she was gone from the earthly plane.

****

Duncan was seated near the shop counter, propped up on his favourite wonky stool. He was starting to think he might have to turn the chair over and fix it himself. He was reading through the event programme for the Folk Festival which didn't give up too much information. It only listed acts, times and included a brief map showing the amenities. But he noted that the headline act at least had a full paragraph of description and a tiny black and white photo.

Banksia was feverishly busy in the roadhouse kitchen out back, preparing readymade take away food for the festival crowd which were expected to be arriving soon. She glanced up at the wall clock and she finally remembered Hannah's lunch order.

"Detective Duncan."

He peered at her over his glasses when he heard his name said.

"Oh shit. I forgot about that bloody hippie diva bird. She wanted me to bring her lunch to her. Would you believe it? I am *so* over it."

"Is she the singer? I think I bumped into her earlier today. She seemed to be a bit of a nervous type to me. Absolutely terrified of nature."

"Yeah. That sounds like her. Look. I'm going to have to duck out for five minutes and take it to her. I'm late by about ten minutes already. She's probably ready to rip right into me."

Duncan shrugged his shoulders and returned to his very light reading, "I can look after things for five minutes. What about the food cooking?"

"You just need to flip the chicken patties over when they're done. Sorry to ask you to do it."

He nodded and said, "I can handle that much. But don't take forever, Banks."

She removed her apron and flicked her eyes to the ceiling, "It's surprising no one's killed her. She's so bloody rude. Anyway, I'd better take her lunch before she *kills* me."

Luckily, she had a steak sandwich prepared earlier and already under the pie warmer. She quickly boiled the kettle and made the lemon tea. She didn't know how strong it had to be, but she made it weak and boiling hot. She didn't like Hannah Dee Wainwright anyway.

Banksia left Detective Duncan in temporary charge of the griller and the roadhouse. He was left to toss the gently sizzling chicken patties for the burgers while she quickly ran her errand.

She raced up the timber decking steps and knocked soundly on the first motel door.

"Lunch is served," she yelled out.

When Hannah Dee Wainwright had not answered her motel room door, Banksia had gone off in search of her, carefully balancing the tray with her lemon tea and steak sandwich. She cursed her under her breath, adding the only audible words 'hippie bloody diva' as she walked swiftly to the only other place the singer could possibly be.

She arrived at the makeshift bathroom she had created.

"Hello? Miss Wainwright. Are you decent?" She cried out, "I've got your lunch right here. Sorry I'm a bit late."

No answer came.

She carefully shrugged the shower curtain aside with a protruding elbow and ducked her head under it. She saw the discarded mini dress and black lace bra on the platform holding the rusty old water tank, but there was no sign of Hannah as she looked around. From what she could see, the bath looked empty. Then she noticed the end of a power cord trailing over the side of the bath. She stepped closer. With one more tentative step she was finally close enough to see into the water and realise what shape she was seeing at the base of the bathtub. Hannah was staring up at her, quiet and still, fully submerged in the bath water. She had jumped back in shook and dropped the tray on the ground in horror. She turned on her heel and ran back to the rear of the roadhouse, screaming.

Duncan heard her and switched off the griller immediately. He was relieved as the chicken patties had started to burn around the edges anyway.

He raced out the back flyscreen door and nearly collided with the hysterical Banksia. She was crying, the tears running abundantly down her round, rosy cheeks and talking so rapidly he could not follow what she was saying. Her hands were visibly shaking.

He grabbed her arms gently and said in his best calming tone, "Slow down. Slow down. Tell me what's wrong."

"It's that hippie diva lady. The singer. She's in the bath and she's not moving," she cried, pulling out of his arms. She was not comfortable with people touching her.

"Where is she?"

"At the water tank around the back, just past the rooms."

"Okay. You stay right here. Did you touch anything?"

She shook her head, "No. No. I'm okay now. I'll come with you."

He jogged ahead, fishing his mobile phone out of his trouser pocket. Banksia walked swiftly behind him.

He roughly pushed the shower curtain aside with an elbow and looked on at the claw foot bath, briefly assessing the scene before him. Banksia finally caught up to him. She stood there next to him, wringing her hands.

"Careful. I think she's been electrocuted," she warned him, stating the obvious.

Duncan stepped forward and peered over the bath edge. He surmised that she had been dead for a while. Too long to be revived. He noted the hair drier on its electrical cord looped over the enamel edge and still dangling in the bath water. His eyes followed the cord across the ground and under the door of the adjacent shed. He lifted up his eyeglasses and rubbed his itchy right eye.

"Yep. She's been deep fried," he sighed and lifted his mobile to his left ear, "I'll have to call it in. Don't touch anything."

"Oh crap. She's dead, isn't she?"

Duncan simply nodded his head and blinked a couple of times behind his glasses.

"She was a real bitch but oh, my god…how awful. Why would she go and kill herself?" She gasped.

"When you got here, did you see anyone else hanging around?"

"No. No one."

"Are your parents at home?" He asked, turning back to look her straight in the eye.

"Of course. They're always at home."

Duncan made a clicking noise with his teeth, "Okay. Well. We'll have to interview everyone on the premises."

As he turned away, he missed seeing Banksia visibly frown and her body stiffen at the thought of her parents being directly approached.

His phone call was answered, "Hey, Rich. Get a unit down here to the Batty Roadhouse as soon as you can. Get forensics across it. I think there's been a murder here. Found her dead in a bathtub."

Duncan was silent for a moment, listening intently to his partner on the other end.

"It's the lead singer at the Folk Festival. Hannah something. Yeah, she's passed away. Looks like it's an accident but I think it's murder. She wasn't exactly little Miss Popular around here. No witnesses either. Not so far anyway."

He stepped away, standing just out of banksia's keen earshot and added in a low voice to Rich, "And right now, I have no ideas on this one. Not yet anyway."

He went quiet again as Rich excitedly told him more bad news.

Duncan rolled his eyes and ranted, "What the hell? Are you kidding me? A whole Latvian mountain rescue team have gone missing in the national park? How does that bloody happen? All we bloody needed. Don't they know how to rescue themselves?"

Chapter Ten

As the forensics team descended on the water tank perimeter with its makeshift bathroom, to fingerprint and thoroughly investigate the crime scene, Banksia was a bundle of nerves. She stood on the side-lines, behind the crime scene tape, nervously chewing on her fingernails. She had locked up the roadhouse and put a hand scrawled sign on the sliding door, 'Back in an hour.' She had already been away much longer than that, but she didn't care. She watched Duncan closely who was confiding in and swapping notes with Detective Richard Bottrell. He had turned up soon after, in the same smart navy suit he always seemed to wear.

When she saw a gap in proceedings, she marched straight up to Duncan. She even reached out to touch his arm which was uncharacteristic of her.

"Detective," she piped up, following him as he briskly power walked away from the crime scene to make an important phone call, "There's something I have to tell you. It's important."

"Banks. The best thing you can do right now is to take me to see your parents. I really need to talk to them."

"Detective. That's just it. You can't speak to them."

Duncan stopped dead in his tracks. He stared at her plump face and raised an eyebrow, "Why is that?"

"Well, you just can't see them."

"Right. You'll have to explain to me why."

She averted her eyes and fidgeted with her hands.

"Because…because they are not really there. In the house. They are not there."

Detective Duncan blinked slowly a few times before grabbing her right elbow and steering her roughly out of earshot of other people milling around them.

"What the fuck do you mean by saying that? Not there? Where are they?"

She freed herself of his tight grasp. She swallowed hard and continued, "It's like I said, my parents are not there. I haven't wanted people around here to know. I think they disappeared about two years ago. A couple of bags and some clothes are missing too, so I just assumed they went away on a holiday. But it's been a long time now and I still haven't heard from either of them. They've gone."

He shook his head and the fingers of his right hand pressed into his forehead, like he had suddenly gained a headache.

"Banks. Are you bloody kidding me? Did you tell the authorities at all? Did you tell anyone else that they were missing?"

"No," she replied, "I'm sorry but I didn't know what to think. They were terrible at running the Batty. I thought they were holidaying. Or maybe, they were so embarrassed by the truth and left to make a new life somewhere else. They had plenty of their own money to do either. My parents were not great communicators after they passed the running of the business to me."

"You know how serious this is."

"Yeah, I think I understand it now."

"But you talked to them, from the kitchen intercom. I saw you. I heard their voices."

She tried to hold back the tears pricking at the corners of her brown eyes.

"What you heard is a recording. I have recorded their voices onto the computer. From years ago. It was from a family Christmas gathering we had."

Duncan cut her off, "Look. I honestly haven't got the time right now to discuss this situation with your parents. And we will need to. I have to make an urgent call to the tour promoter to see what to do about this music festival. Can't turn the crowds away now."

"What do I do, in the meantime?"

"Just go back to the roadhouse, keep on working. I'll come and see you much later."

She stepped forward and asked in a scared, small voice, "Are you going to tell the other detective about…what we've discussed?"

He shook his head, "No. Not yet. But I will have to. You understand? Your parents are missing, Banks. They may even be dead."

She looked ready to burst into tears, so he patted her arm and gave her a reassuring smile.

He raced off to find a quiet place to make the call. In the end, he parked himself behind the shed and unfurled the crumpled festival brochure with the phone number scrawled across it.

He dialled with speed and was quite surprised to get Tour Promoter Des Rundall on the line right away.

"Des Rundall? I'm Senior Detective Phillip Duncan. I am contacting you from Beecham's Bridge National Park."

"Oh yeah? What can I do you for, detective?" He replied, sounding like he was halfway through a yawn.

"I am very sorry to inform you, but your star performer Hannah Dee Wainwright has met with a fatal accident. She's dead unfortunately. And I guess we need to know…is this festival to proceed? A lot of people are already here and the stall holders are all set up, for the market."

Des dropped his mobile phone and Duncan heard it clutter across a hard floor. A minute passed by before he responded.

"Goddamn it, really? Can't believe it. She was a real trooper. Well, yes, the show must go on. Can you find someone to fill in? A busker, anyone with a good enough voice?"

"Mate, that's not my job. I think you have to call someone who's here, your organisers. Anyway, I'm sorry for your loss."

He wasn't sure but it sounded like the promoter was crying, "How did she die?"

He asked quietly.

"I'm afraid I can't say. Need to investigate more. We will need to catch up soon."

"Of course, of course. Only too happy to cooperate with the authorities, detective."

Duncan closed the call.

On the other end, Des was seated at his large ornate desk in his low-rise Melbourne office. He wiped a tear away on his cheek and taped his fountain pen on the desk surface. He was not a fan of last-minute changes, and he knew he stood to lose a lot of money if he pulled the plug on the event one hour before the first performance. The thought of handing back over one thousand ticket refunds prompted him to take immediate action.

He dialled Brody's number, "Hey, buddy, we have a situation. You know Hannah's gone and carked it. Talk about bad timing. Are there any buskers around at the festival?"

He listened for a long minute and then replied, "Pull yourself together, lad. The show must go on."

Brody continued to talk excitedly and Des nodded his head as he listened intently. Finally, he said, " Righto. She can sing okay? She knows the songs too? Oh yeah? Okay, she'll have to do. Tell her it's worth five hundred bucks to her. She can camp in Hannah's motel room too. Brody, go save the day, my man. I trust your good judgement."

****

"Misty Rae Phoenix. Bloody hell, now that's not your real name, is it?" Duncan smirked. He was fidgeting, picking up a small open pot of gold glitter eyeshadow. He placed it down again.

Misty Rae said nothing and bit down on her bottom lip. She had been busy standing in front of the small square mirror in the makeup tent offstage, fixing her fine hair braids and readjusting the array of beads, feathers and strings of leather attached to her wild brown hair. She had also changed her brown leather vest to a red leather bustier. If she was going to be onstage, she wanted to look her hippie best. Her ankle length floral pleated skirt just hid her bare feet and her jangling ankle bracelets.

She smiled up at the senior detective and tugged the chest bow of her bustier just a bit tighter. Her tits squashed up further, which she quite liked the look of. Duncan nodded his head slightly, as if he liked it too.

She flicked her eyes to look at him briefly, "I don't know if I can do this, take her place. It's a lot of pressure."

"I understand why you are hesitant. I really do," he said in an unusually quieter tone for him, "but you have your chance to shine. Your moment in the sun."

"Yeah sure. It's a dream come true."

Duncan smirked and leaned back against a tent pole, folding his arms across his chest.

"What a fortunate turn of events for you. The main act drops conveniently dead just hours *before* the big concert," he said drily.

Misty Rae refreshed her charcoal black matte lipstick and glared at him through the mirror, "Hey, I'm not that desperate for fame that I have to kill someone. I really admire Hannah Dee Wainwright. I mean, I admired her. She was a ballsy lady in this tough industry."

"So people keep telling me."

"This is a one-off gig for me. To save the show. Her band asked me if I would help them out. I said I would."

Brody stuck his head with its unruly mop of brown hair through the tent flap.

"Hey. We're on in five minutes," he announced, "you think you'll be ready?"

She gave him a thumbs up.

Duncan unfurled himself from the tent pole and said,

"Break a leg."

He slipped out, with the intention of leaving her to prepare for the performance.

She heaved a sigh and sat down at the makeshift dressing table, where Hannah had recently sat as well. She studied her face in the tiny face mirror and added a touch more rouge to her cheeks with a fingertip dipped in the blusher. She nervously took a swig of gin and tonic which the stage manager had thoughtfully brought her.

She sat quietly before picking up her bespoke guitar and slinging its strap overhead and across her chest.

Misty Rae Phoenix visibly shook off stage. This was something new and confronting for her.

She was accustomed to basking in the streets to a handful of strangers who found it hard to part with their loose change, but performing on a huge festival stage was vastly different. This was the moment she had been waiting for all her fifty years. While she felt sorry for Hannah, she was grateful for her chance to fill her designer shoes.

The MC spoke excitedly into the microphone to the crowd and raised his left hand high for quiet.

"Sorry, folks, Hannah Dee Wainwright is unable to perform for us tonight. I know you've been waiting patiently for her," he announced. The one thousand and one strong crowd collectively moaned.

"But there's some good news. We have another very talented lady who will perform with Hannah's band. Introducing Misty Rae Phoenix."

Right on cue, she strode out across the bendy particleboard stage, holding her guitar out and fronted the band. Brody clutched his guitar, his eyes swollen red from tears. Hannah's sudden demise had hit him the hardest. Greg peeped out behind the drum set looked weary from all the grog he had consumed while Davo drummed his fingers on the top of his organ, waiting anxiously to start.

She heard a few people clapping but it died off too quickly. Then she only heard birdsong. She turned briefly to the band and said, "I'll lead off, just follow me. The key is G flat, okay?"

Her pitchy, high shrill voice rose above their bad, discordant playing. She knew Hannah's one big hit song and did her own rendition of it. She slowed it down a fraction in the middle, leading into the repeat of the chorus. The band managed to keep the pace.

Then she sang four more songs, well-known folk songs which carried them to the end of their stage performance.

The crowd whistled and clapped wildly. Misty Rae was forced to return and present one more song, and she choose a cover Hannah loved to sing. This time, the band lost their place halfway through as Greg's music sheets had blown away, taken by a sudden gust of wind. She ended the performance with just her searing vocals and the gentle strumming of her bespoke guitar. The crowd clapped along with some enthusiastic leading from Brody who had started to enjoy himself. She waved her hand to the appreciative audience and strode off stage as the comedy act waltzed past her, with his own entourage in hot pursuit, fluffing up his feather fringed sequin suit.

"Thank god, that's over," she sighed, struggling with the guitar strap and finally pulling it up and over her head. Her beaded hair strands gently rapped against it in the struggle.

She swiftly walked past Duncan who was standing in the wings, making his mental notes.

"You looked quite good up there, very at ease," he remarked.

"Detective. Busking is easy, but this shit's so fuckin' hard."

"Miss, Misty Rae, before you go, I still need to interview you. We can do it now or later. I hope you plan to be around tomorrow."

She turned and looked up at his intense blue eyes. She nodded, "I haven't got plans for this evening, but I think I will do something interesting. It's been a bit of a big day. But I promise you I will be around, and I keep my promises. Okay? Am I free to go now?"

"Of course."

He stood to one side. letting her pass with her guitar strapped across her chest.

As he watched her jump down from the stage, his mobile started to ring.

"Hey, Rich. What's up?"

He listened intently for a few moments.

"Oh wow. The Latvian Mountain rescue team have just turned up? They've been watching the folk concert? I guess that's one worry ticked off our bucket list, Rich."

As Detective Duncan continued talking animatedly on his mobile, Misty Rae had turned the corner and walked past the security office.

Ricardo came out, having finished his work shift, and handed in his security pass for the night. He recognised Misty Rae as she strode by and followed her.

"Hey, babe. Wait up," he yelled out.

She turned her head and half smiled at him, "Hey hello. Had a bit of a night. I'm going to bed to sleep."

He finally caught up to her and he had to catch his breath. He managed to say.

"Hey, come on. Bloody hell, babe. The night's still young. Why don't you come back to my caravan and we have a little fun? Or fuck, we could just talk. Whatever you wanna do. You were great up there, on the stage."

"Thanks..umm."

"I'm Rick. Remember?"

"Oh yes, Sorry."

"And hey, I invited a couple of girls over too. Maybe we can have a foursome, hey?"

Misty Rae stopped in mid stride and studied him. Middle aged short, stocky men with salt and pepper hair was not a type she was usually interested in, but he was pleasant and friendly enough. She screwed up her face and then sighed, "After what's happened tonight, I guess…why not? Let's have an orgy party then."

Ricardo couldn't believe his luck. He ran his blunt spatula fingers through his grey peppered hair and scratched his prominent roman nose.

"Well, alright," he exclaimed excitedly, "this way."

His caravan was parked in a dirt and gravel carpark usually reserved for hikers' parked vehicles. It was not the only one there, as several other festival goers had set up camp there too. Ricardo's mobile home was basic and cosy. Misty Rae had a foreboding feeling that it was not very soundproof either.

He lunged forward and quickly unlocked the door with a flourish. Then he stepped back like a gentleman and let her go first inside. But as she climbed the two tiny steps, she felt his hand slap her backside which was quite a feat in itself as he strategically just missed hitting her guitar. The firm slap surprised her, but she decided not to slap him back.

Once inside, he became an absolute gentleman again, helping her into the bench chair at the narrow kitchen table and fussing over her with a plateful of nibbles from his caravan fridge and setting up his coffee percolator.

"No, please no coffee for me. Not into coffee," she said, putting up her hand. She removed the guitar strap over her head and rested her treasured instrument against the wall behind her.

"Oh wow, okay. How about a stiff drink then? I got a bottle of gin, and I got some expensive pinot noir shit from the Barossa Valley. I bought it 'cos it had a fuckin' nice picture on the label. See? How nice is that picture? Real classy wine for a classy lady singer. You could become famous after tonight."

She smiled shyly, "Naw. It's not going to happen now at my age. Please. Don't tease me about it."

"But you're unreal up there on the stage. I couldn't fucking take my eyes off you."

Just then, there was a loud rapping sound on the side of the caravan.

Ricardo winked at her and said, "It's okay. It's the other girls, right on time. Hold your thoughts."

The two twenty-somethings pulled themselves up the side steps and walked in, casually dressed.

The blonde with short, bobbed hair said, "Hi, I'm Karen."

The redhead with curly shoulder length hair said, "Hey, I'm Taylor."

"Howdy. Make yourself at home, ladies." Ricardo spun around, excited, "Oh fuck. This is beautiful. Just beautiful. This is Misty, the singer."

Misty Rae looked up at the twenty-somethings but said nothing. She only nodded her acknowledgement. Ricardo jumped onto his double bed in the other corner and lay on his side, positioning himself for the best view.

"What do you ladies want to drink? Gin or this real expensive wine I bought?"

The blonde smiled and said, "I don't drink."

"I'm a vegetarian," the redhead added.

"Come on, ladies. Show us what you got. I wanna see some titties."

The blonde and the redhead turned to each other and giggled. Together, they pulled their t-shirts up over their heads and proudly showed off their bare, voluptuous breasts. Misty Rae stood up and went to put her hands up to her red bustier. She started to pull down on the front zip, showing the upper round curves of her pert small breasts.

Ricardo raised his hand, "Whoa, babe. You're a special lady to me. I think you should join in last. Come here, my young lovelies."

The blonde and the redhead eagerly rushed forward and surrounded him either side on the bed. The caravan lurched onto one side and Misty Rae had to adjust her balance to keep upright.

Ricardo's brown eyes widen, and he felt each ample, soft breast he was offered and sucked hard on a nipple here and there. It was like a long-time fantasy come true for him. He couldn't stop grinning from ear to ear.

"Oh wow, girls, you're doing just great," he started to enthusiastically rub his penis which was starting to get rock hard. The redhead smiled and her right hand went to help him dislodge his cock from his trousers.

Suddenly, Ricardo diverted his hand and rubbed his left chest instead, his eyes widen in a mixture of pain and ecstasy. With his mouth wide open, he rolled onto his stomach, his face falling flat into the pillow. He didn't appear to move after that.

Misty Rae who had stopped the start of her strip tease for him, frowned and took a tentative step forward.

"Hey, Rick," she called out to his prone figure. There was no response.

She took a tentative step forward. The younger women giggled again between themselves but then realised the seriousness of the moment and stopped abruptly. Their eyes widened and the blonde dramatically cupped her hand over her rose bud lips.

"Oh, my god. You've got to be frigging kidding me?" Misty Rae exclaimed, hands on hip. She turned to face the younger women, "He's dead. He's gone and carked it on us. I can't believe how my night's turned out."

Chapter Eleven

The folk concert was halfway through its acts by eleven o'clock. Banksia was seated in the roadhouse kitchen, dabbing tissues under her eyes. She could hear the pulsating beats and feel the soft vibrations of the music in the distance. She was thinking about her missing parents and the realisation that they were in fact missing, had finally hit her hard. Her eye make-up had run. She rarely wore make-up, but she reasoned to herself that the music festival might lead the 'one' she was waiting for straight to her doorstep. She was wearing lots of mascara and thick black eyeliner. She had even let her light brown hair down to roll over her broad shoulders. Regardless of her concerted efforts to dazzle, she still looked plain.

Now that she had locked the front door to customers, the future love of her life was unlikely to turn up. Her eyes were starting to swell from the steady stream of tears and turn red, and she blew her nose for the tenth consecutive time.

She thought about putting the kettle on and making a cup of green tea for herself, to calm her nerves when her mobile rang next to her elbow. Banksia picked it up with no hesitation as she already knew who the caller was.

"Detective Duncan," she answered, her voice quivering a little.

"Yes, it is me. Sorry, I have been busy with all this craziness at the festival. But now, we need to get serious," his voice was firm and authoritarian, but sounded tired at the same time.

"I understand, just let me know when you are here, and I'll let you in."

"You're at the roadhouse? Okay. Detective Bottrell will be coming along with me."

Banksia let out an audible gasp, "Is that necessary?"

"He's my partner. We'll be there in five minutes, Banks."

The line hung up.

She took a fresh tissue out of the box on the table and blew her nose hard. She stood up, had a bit of a stretch and straightened her t-shirt. She walked slowly towards the glass doors and by the time she reached them, Duncan and Bottrell were standing there. Both were wearing their best suits, but minus ties.

She unlocked the sliding doors and the detectives stepped inside quickly.

"Let's get a look at the house."

She nodded and pointed towards the kitchen, "It's best to walk out the back way."

They followed her out into the cool night air, Bottrell switching on his flashlight. They only had to work twenty-five metres to the early nineteen-hundreds built cottage with a return veranda. The flashlight was not necessary as they walked under the silvery glow of the full moon, and the fairy lights around the concert area twinkled and danced through the trees ahead.

Duncan was the first to step up onto the veranda and it creaked loudly under his footfall, and he noticed the weathered timber posts and the chipped paint on the door and window frames. He swept a long index finger over the dusty door handle.

"Needs a lot of work here," he muttered. His shoe made a crunching sound, and he took his foot off and backed up. Rich responded by switching on his flashlight.

The light shone on a large mound of dead dried blowfly corpses which his foot had settled on.

Banksia who was standing next to Duncan's elbow was oblivious to the flies and explained, "My parents are academic types, they're not handy at all."

Rich sniffed the air, "Can you smell that? Something smells a bit off. Don't you reckon?"

"Banks, when was the last time you went inside the house?"

She dabbed at the corners of her eyes with a fresh tissue and fished the front door key from her apron pocket.

"I don't know. But maybe about eighteen months ago. I opened the door for a few seconds and then closed it. There are probably mice running around inside. I don't like mice. That's the smell most probably."

"Could be. Let's have a good look around, Rich."

The door creaked open a fraction. She gave it a firm shove with her right shoulder. Banksia stuck her hand inside to flick the power switch on. The hallway light flickered a couple of times before flooding the area with light. The bare globe which hung down on a long electrical cord, made a consistent buzzing noise. Duncan stepped inside, the polished Baltic pine floorboards groaning a little under foot and he immediately covered his nose.

"Wow. It's strong, whatever the smell is."

Bottrell did the same, followed by Banksia who entered last, pinching her wide nostrils together.

Duncan turned to look at her, "Don't touch anything, okay?"

She pointed her right hand down the end of the hallway, "My parents used to spend most of their time in the study, on their computers. Or they were watching television in the living room. That's the room on the left."

Still holding his nose, Duncan looked up at the pressed metal ceilings, admiring them and then cast his eyes over the canary yellow painted hallway. When he looked at Banksia again, she looked a little more relaxed. He found she was easy to read. She stopped at every painting and picture in the hallway, the family memories flooding back to her.

The detectives walked together into the study. The leatherette swivel office chairs were well worn, and still had human indents in the seats. Duncan could see the pair of them had been big people. The chairs were positioned to face two very dusty computer screens and keyboards. Duncan took out a tissue from his trouser pocket and picked up a photo frame on one of the desks. It was a picture of Banksia in her school uniform, flanked by her parents Janine and Bob. Everyone was smiling into the lens. He placed it down gently. She appeared and stared at the photo frame over his elbow. He turned his head enough to see that her eyes were misting over.

"That's mum and dad."

"Tell me, Banks. What happened that day? The day that you realised they weren't here in the house anymore?"

She swallowed hard, "Oh okay. I remember it was the end of the day. I came over to see them. I had made them a batch of fish and chips, their favourite. But when I got here, the front door was wide open. I looked everywhere inside for them, nothing. But I did find mum's wardrobe was open and a lot of her clothes had gone. It was strange. But dad had left me a note. I found it on the kitchen bench, between the salt and pepper shakers. I nearly didn't see it."

"A note? Where's this note?"

She pointed a thumb in the direction of the roadhouse, "Of course I've kept it. Show you later. But basically, the note said they went away for a bit of a break."

Rich had been walking around the kitchen and he stepped back into the study.

"I was just thinking…is there a cellar somewhere, Lovey?" He asked.

Banksia shrugged her shoulders, "I don't remember. I don't know actually. Maybe there's one."

Rich cleared his throat with his wheezy smoker's cough and said directly to Duncan.

"Considering its age, I'm sure this old house has a cellar and it might be worth me looking for it."

His partner nodded his head. They separated in the hallway, with Duncan heading into her parents' bedroom and Banksia too, following close behind. He stood at the foot of their queen size bed with a dusty floral quilt over it. He could hear the patter of mice within the walls somewhere. The dressing table and its trinkets were covered in a thick layer of dust and he saw the opened wardrobe. He peered in and noticed there was a sizeable empty gap where clothing had been hanging.

"Let me understand this. You saved their voices?"

"Yeah, I'd recorded them in the past. I set up everything on the computer. It was easy. I've rigged it so there's a call every day to the kitchen phone. I know it sounds crazy, but it made me feel comfortable. If I believed they were still here…it stopped my panic attacks happening. When I found they had gone, well, as you would understand, I was anxious and upset. I was all over the place and…"

While Duncan listened to Banksia's long-winded explanation, Rich had been busy moving furniture and lifting up rugs in every room. He entered the last bedroom which was more of a junk room filled with boxes and old sewing machines. He struggled to push things off the rug in the middle of the floor and finally managed it on his fourth attempt. He dusted his hands on his previously clean trousers and was pleased to find a hatch for the cellar. He gripped the embedded brass handle and raised the lid. As soon as it opened, a layer of fine dust rose up, filling the air and a terrible smell hit his nostrils. He recoiled for a moment, coughed and held his nose with the fingers of his left hand. With his right, he pulled out his flashlight which was hooked on his trouser belt and flicked it on. He shone the light downwards and found the side ladder leading into the cellar depths.

He carefully climbed down, and jump landed onto the dirt floor with his good leather shoes. He regretted his hasty move, as a cloud of dust rose and covered them. He still held his nose tight, and whirled around the cellar, pointing the flashlight but it was hard to focus as his eyes were not accustomed to the dark. As he panned it around, he saw a shaft of light and he could just make out shapes in the far-left corner. It looked like a slither of moonlight was beaming in from a small, broken window high up.

He stepped forward and the flashlight grasped in his hand glowed brighter. He suddenly stopped in his tracks and took a shaky step backwards. The torch illuminated two badly decomposing bodies lying slumped against each other. The flesh hung in black strips, and what was left of it on the bones. A stream of mice scattered across the floor in all directions, which genuinely made him jump.

He tried not to gag and raced back to the ladder. He climbed out superfast for a man nearing retirement age and quickly dropped the latch door onto the cellar with a thud. The terrible smell of rotting flesh hung in the air around him. He bent over, his hands clutching his knees and he let another smoker's cough go. When he had gathered his thoughts, he stood up and went looking for his partner.

He found him in the parents' bedroom, still discussing her decision not to advise the authorities of their disappearance.

"Hey, mate," Rich leaned in, indicating with the shake of his head to follow him.

"Excuse me for just a moment," Duncan said.

He followed Rich into the kitchen and closed the door. There were mouse droppings all over the kitchen benchtops and Duncan was trying hard to ignore it. Rich slouched against the fridge and straightened his jacket. Duncan noted his partner's demeanour was serious and his facial expression solemn.

"I reckon I've found them. I've found her parents. They're dead, lying dead in the cellar. That's the smell of death hanging in the air. Been dead for quite some time too. There's a broken window in the cellar which I think's recent. Explains all the blowies hanging around. We've got another crime scene on our hands."

Duncan folded his arms across his chest and averted his eyes to the lino floor.

"Fucking hell," he groaned the words, removed his glasses and rubbed his eyes.

"But I fucked up too, mate."

He paused to let out a dry smoker's cough.

"How?"

"I went down into the cellar and my fingerprints would be on the goddamn ladder now. Didn't think twice about it. I hope we can still get the killer's prints off it."

Banksia's face peered auspiciously around the kitchen door. Rich saw the terrified, hurt look in her soft brown eyes and knew instantly that she had heard him say the words she had feared ever hearing. He stood straight and breezed past Detective Duncan who was still contemplating the new circumstances.

Rich patted her plump arm and steered her gently towards the front door.

"Lovey, I think it might be best for you to wait for us outside. We'll be with you in a few minutes, okay? I promise you."

Banksia looked hurt but she obeyed him. She turned with her shoulders slightly hunched. She walked down the hallway and left quietly.

"So, do you think the bodies are of Janine and Bob Peterson?"

Rich nodded his head, "Dead certain. Who else would they be? They were in the house all this time, they never bloody left it, mate."

"Fuck," Duncan let out a big, long sigh, "bloody hell. They're dropping dead like flies around here. I think I found a bullet hole in the wall behind the desk. It had a bad patch up paint job. I'm sure it's a bullet hole."

"Hey, Phil," Rich lowered his voice a couple of notches and asked him very quietly, "about the young lady. You don't seriously buy her supreme act of innocence. Do you?"

Duncan swivelled around on his right heel, "Yeah. Actually, I do. You just said it straight out. She's still young, you know. She's a bit naïve perhaps. But she's definitely not a killer. She loved her parents, that's obvious."

"I really need to see her father's note."

Duncan took out his small notebook from his back trouser pocket, "Wait a sec. Before we go outside, we might have a visual of the actual killer. Banks showed me the security cameras. And there was one camera installed in the house in the kitchen."

His partner smirked and straightened his jacket, "Well, I'm about to retire, as you well know. I don't mind going through the surveillance footage in the office. If you want me to. Someone's got to do it. At least I get to rest my arse."

****

Kimberley was straddling Duncan's hips, leaning back and concentrating on the singular pursuit of her own pleasure. He had already come, and he was mesmerised, studying her naked form as she closed her eyes tight and tossed her long hair back. Her breasts gently jiggled above him, and he reached out to tease her hard, pointed nipples. Finally, she screamed out and her whole body shunted. The entire caravan seemed to rock on its suspension as she did.

Breathing hard, she leant over his chest, and they kissed deeply, his tongue probing and hungry for her own. He gently thrust a forefinger into her and twirled it around her swollen clitoris. She gasped and whimpered deep in her throat, quite enjoying his touch.

Then she rolled onto the bed, on his right side and nestled her face under his musky armpit. Her long blonde hair spread out over her neck and across his naked abdomen. Duncan stared into her irresistible doe eyes which were looking up at him. She smiled sweetly and his heart felt like it was going to burst out of his chest.

He kissed the top of her forehead.

"Phil, how many times was that?" She asked him.

He shrugged his shoulders, "I don't know. I've lost count of all our orgasms."

She laughed and said, "I think it's ten but not sure."

"What time is it? I'm getting hungry. Do you feel like having some breakfast?"

Kimberley glanced momentarily at her wristwatch, "It's three o'clock in the afternoon. Missed breakfast now. It's lunchtime. No. It's past lunchtime. We might as well go to dinner soon."

Duncan grimaced, playing with her hair, "You're joking. We've been lying in here for hours. I should be working, you know. You need to stop distracting me, honey."

"I'm distracting you? No one's come looking for you. So far anyway, they haven't."

Duncan put his left arm up over his head and sighed heavily.

"It was a big night. I'm happy this concert business is over and done with."

Suddenly, there was a loud rapping sound against the caravan door and a man's voice yelling out his name.

"Okay. That's the end of our harmony, looks like it. Stay right here. I think it's my partner knocking."

He rolled out of bed and reached for his bathrobe to conceal his semi erection and nakedness. He grabbed his discarded eyeglasses from off the floor. After rubbing his eyes, he popped his glasses on the bridge of his nose. He gripped the door handle and awkwardly slid down the steel steps outside.

Detective Bottrell stood there in the clearing, hands on hips, looking serious in his favourite suit.

"Hey, Rich, mate, what's up?"

Rich flicked his eyes around, "Glad to see that some people can sleep half the day away. While you were…doing whatever you were doing in there, I've been hard at work. I only got a couple of hours of sleep myself."

Duncan yawned loudly and scratched the back of his neck. Then his hand wandered to his chin, and he felt the stubble which had appeared overnight.

"Okay. You've been working on the murders of Banksia's parents and the diva."

"And all the rest. Anyway, you know," he inclined his head for a moment, wishing he hadn't said it, "oh yeah. You missed even some more excitement last night. We've got another dead body to deal with."

"What the fuck?" He exclaimed.

"But we don't think it's a murder. You can relax. Just some poor middle-aged fella died of a heart attack while the concert was on. It wasn't reported straight away either. I think it was embarrassing for all the people involved."

"People?"

"Yeah. The police were called. They turned up and found two young topless women and your busker friend there with this guy's body in his caravan. I'm putting my bets on some hanky-panky maybe. Half his luck. What a way to go."

"Crap. That's four dead in a short time. I don't like it. Don't like it at all."

"Mate. The heart attack man is nothing to worry about. But I bought you his picture anyway."

Rich reached into his inside jacket pocket and pulled out the photograph. He passed it to Duncan who studied it closely and raised an eyebrow.

"Oh wow, I actually know this guy. It's been a couple of years, but he was working in the construction business. He was staying in Brumby Flat for a short time. When the series of murders happened a couple of years back. But I can't remember his name."

Rich shook his head, "Well, Ricardo something. Anyway, he was working as a security guard here at the festival. I had to tell his poor wife in Adelaide. It wasn't an easy thing to do. And head office wanted to know what you're up to. They told me they've tried to contact you. But I covered for you. I said you were investigating a couple of leads. I didn't say you were…investigating your new girlfriend."

"Hey. Don't bring my Kimberley into this," Duncan growled and added, "I'll get dressed and we'll go see Banks first. There are still some unanswered questions right there."

"Yeah. For sure."

Rich turned to leave but Duncan reached out and tapped his arm, "By the way, thanks for the kind loan of your caravan."

"Just remember that I want it back the day *before* I actually retire. Not long to go now. Can't wait to go camping and fishing."

Chapter Twelve

Banksia Peterson sat at the shop counter of the Batty Roadhouse, typing furiously away on her laptop. Apart from a couple of road trains travelling through and stopping for a tank of fuel, she had nothing much to do. It had been an unusually quiet day. She had cleaned the kitchen and cooked up some takeaway hamburgers and hot chips for the passing evening trade who would be appearing soon.

A week had passed since the folk festival and the bodies of her parents had been found in the basement of their cottage. She had closed the Batty Roadhouse for a few days after the festival, just to give herself some time to adjust to this tragic news and deal with the change in her personal circumstances. She had, after all, inherited the roadhouse.

She tucked a stray dark strand of hair behind her left ear. Somehow it had escaped her tight bun. She was busy sending emails and private messages. She smiled and giggled at the last message received.

Duncan suddenly breezed in, and she looked up from the screen. Reluctantly, she closed the laptop lid.

"Hi, Banks. I need to get some petrol today."

She got up, straightened her apron and tapped her fingers lightly over the console, "Card or cash? By the way, you might as well be the first person to know about my plans. I'm leaving the Batty."

Duncan briefly raised his eyes from his wallet, "I've got the cash. What? You're leaving us?"

Banksia swallowed hard, "Yeah. I've thought long and hard about it and since…my parents are gone now, I don't have a good reason to stay here anymore."

"Wow. I don't understand. Where will you go? Are you selling the roadhouse?"

"Oh god, no. It's been in our family for too long. I'm just going to find someone to run it for me, while I move to America."

"America? All the way to America?"

"Yes. I've been talking to this amazing guy over in the states. We started chatting on this dating site. He wants to meet me so I think I'll take the risk and fly over to Miami."

"You can't just drop everything and leave."

She rolled her shoulders, "Why ever not?"

"Because I think we're closing in on the murderer. That's why. I still have your father's last note."

"That's okay. When you finish with it, I'll give you a forwarding address. Look, I need to move on and start enjoying my life again, Phil. I've just been working seven days a week, thinking my parents were still alive out there. What a silly little fool I've been. It's time for me to grow up."

Her brown eyes started to tear up in the corners and Duncan reached into his pocket to hand her a clean handkerchief. She took it, saying a quiet thank you. She wiped them gently away and looked into his vivid blue eyes.

"You know, you've been very kind to me, Phil. Like a good friend. I really needed a friend through all this."

"It's okay, Banks. I've enjoyed our friendship too. But I wasn't good enough in your kitchen," he said with a grin.

"Ah. You did well enough. You were great at burning all my sausages and meat patties."

He indicated with his thumb outside, "My partner Rich is coming inside soon. We still need to complete that interview with you. I would like to get the last questions I have out of the way today."

They could see through the shop window Rich standing at the petrol pump filling up his impressive expensive car.

She nodded, "Do I have to come into the police station again?"

"No. It's okay. Just a few more questions. We can do it here."

"Oh yeah. I'm interviewing staff over the next couple of days. Two sound really perfect. Both of them happen to live in your town Brumby Flat."

"When have you booked your flights?"

"I'm not going right away, Phil. I have to tidy up things. It will take me a few weeks to sort it all out. Might be months yet."

Rich walked in and had his wallet already out.

"Hi, Lovey," he said brightly, handing over a crisp fifty dollar note.

She opened the register and issued him change.

Banksia turned her head at the beeping sound coming from the kitchen intercom.

"I have to go to the weighbridge for a customer. Take a seat at a table. I'll join you soon."

Rich and Duncan stepped into the dining room and selected a table.

"She knows we have to question her?" Rich asked.

"Yeah, she does. She also just told me that she's leaving the Batty Roadhouse."

"What? I didn't see that coming."

They waited patiently for ten minutes.

Finally, she breezed back in and joined them at the table.

Rich spoke first, "I hear you're leaving us."

"I'm not going to leave right away. It will take me weeks to sort everything out. I have to spend time training new staff to take over. I have to pack my parents gear away. Will have to arrange storage too."

"I have a copy of the note left in the house by your father. Can you handle me reading it to you now?"

She visibly shivered and clasped her hands on the table,

"Yes, I think I can handle it. Go ahead."

Rich cleared his dry throat, "Banksia dear, I must commend you on the great job of managing the roadhouse. Your mother and I have decided to take a long break. Don't worry about us, my dear. We're going to travel around the country. All our love."

Duncan took over and said, "Now see his handwriting here. It's very shaky. I think he was forced to write it by whoever murdered them. What made you think it was a legitimate note? Why did you believe everything the message said?" she wiped more tears away, "I don't know. Because I'm his daughter."

She clutched her chest, "Why wouldn't I believe his words? My parents were very private people, nothing really surprised me about them. And when I went into the house and saw their clothes and some personal stuff gone, I had no cause to think anything terrible had happened to them."

"Okay."

"I want to see whoever is responsible for the murders of my parents brought to justice. I hope you are close to finding them."

"We think so. We believe your parents were getting close to some local truths themselves."

"They were clever people."

Duncan took her outstretched right hand and gently squeezed it for a moment.

"Yes, they were. And don't forget that, Banks. You should be proud of them. There were a couple of interesting files saved on their computers. We believe they were doing their own research to produce a history of Beecham's Bridge. Unfortunately, it might have cost them their lives."

Banksia's bottom lip began to quiver, and she burst into a steady stream of tears.

Rich was a tough old bugger. However, her teary reaction tugged at Rich's heart so much, he got up out of his chair and squatted down next to her. He placed his hand gently on her shoulder.

"It's okay, Lovey," he said in a low soothing tone of voice, "I know it's an awful lot to take in."

She took a deep breath, "You don't understand, detective. My parents were on a different level to me. They were university scholars, and I never went to uni. I only finished high school. I think they were ashamed of me, especially my father."

Rich leaned in, sharing the screen of his mobile phone with her, "No. No. You're wrong. Look at this. See the first words that your father wrote in his note? He opens with 'I commend you on the great job of managing the roadhouse.'

He wasn't forced to write that sentence. That was the way he talked, right? I think this sentence right here is his last great gift to you. He wrote that especially for you, in praise of you."

She was still crying but she nodded her head in understanding, "I guess you're right. They really had no idea how to run this place. They were too academic to deal with customers."

"See? There you are."

Duncan jumped in and said, "I think we're all done now. Thanks for your cooperation, Banks."

"No problem."

She walked off, back to the shop counter, dabbing at her eyes with a tissue from her apron pocket.

When she was out of earshot, Rich turned in his chair to his partner.

"So, what do you think now?"

Duncan grimaced, "Yes, she's innocent. Definitely. I hope we can find this serial killer who's running wild out here. Far out, Rich. We have five people dead. They're dropping like bloody flies."

"Yeah, mate. So you keep on saying. It's not good. And I'm supposed to be retiring soon."

"I meant to ask you earlier, but did you manage to get through the video footage from the Peterson's kitchen?"

"Yeah, mate," Rich's whole demeanour changed, and he looked solemn. "There's nothing on it. Just them cooking and walking about the kitchen. Hours and hours of nothing but. They weren't killed in the kitchen for sure. Forensics reckon Janine and Bob Peterson were both shot down in the cellar. No actually, that's not right. The report says Janine was killed inside the house, in the hallway. Poor bloke was killed in the cellar. If that's the case, Banks probably heard nothing from the roadhouse. Their house is a bit of a distance away from the business."

"Has to be a local."

Rich snorted, "Could also be someone who knows the park really well, like a regular passer-by. Do you reckon? But I hope not."

"Rich, you're a good bloke you know. You were very good with Banks just then. She needed to hear what you said to her."

His older partner rolled his shoulders and replied, "Hey, I'm kind when I have to be, and cruel when I need to be."

****

Duncan was tapping the keys on his laptop in the caravan. Kimberley was busy in the other corner, seated on the bed, checking and sending text messages to friends on her mobile phone. They had not been together as a couple for very long, but she knew well enough when he needed space and alone time to do his work.

Suddenly, he cried out and swore. She looked up for a brief moment and noticed he had changed his positioning. He had his elbows square on the table and his hands were clutching the top of his balding, close shaven head. His intense blue eyes were downcast. He had even closed his laptop up and pushed it roughly aside on the narrow dining table.

Concerned, she uncrossed her legs and arose from the bed. She was still dressed in her pyjamas since the morning. She left her mobile languishing on the doona cover, lost somewhere in a fold.

"What is it, Phil? Are you okay?"

He shook his head a little, "No, not really. This is a crock of shit. I need extra help from my department to sort this bloody mess out, but I can't get it. My partner's going to retire soon. Then what happens? I'll be on my own, of course. I'll be left here, with bodies up to my bloody eyeballs to sort out."

She manoeuvred herself behind him and pressed her hands over his shoulders which felt tight and she started to slowly massage them. Her mane of long, straight blonde hair brushed his left cheek. As she let her fingers fly and work their magic, he closed his eyes and removed his glasses. He cleared his dry throat.

He arched his back and sighed, "Ah yeah. That feels nice, Kimberley. Just what I needed right now."

"I don't understand why they can't give you the resources you need," she whispered close to his ear.

"I think I'm not coping too well. Sorry. Got a lot of worries in my head, my love. It's not your fault and nothing you can do about it."

"Phil, maybe you need to go home to Brumby Flat. And relax for a while."

Duncan smirked and reached over his other shoulder to clasp her hand.

"If I go home, I'll keep thinking of my dead wife, Bette. If I stay here at the national park, I'll think of my murdered parents. I don't have any peace at the moment anywhere, not until I find this killer. I need to find them before they kill again."

He very gently kissed her hand and she leaned against his back, enveloping him in a warm, tight hug, "I love you. I wish I could help you more."

"You help me just by being here, that's more than enough for me," he said.

"Can I please say something?"

He nodded his head.

"Anything. Go for it. What's on your mind?"

"What if the killer or killers of your parents are not here anymore. It was a long time ago. Maybe you are dealing with a new killer out here."

Duncan sighed heavily and drummed his fingers lightly across the table.

"No. My gut's telling me the killer's still around here. They are close by."

"Come on, Phil. Come back to bed. I think you need a short break from your work."

He patted her forearm and smirked, "Sounds like a good plan, my love."

Chapter Thirteen

Her voice came down through the phone line a bit breathless and Old Chook felt he was obliged to offer his assistance to her immediately. He stood up from his unkempt kitchen table and tried to stretch out the crick in his back. A veteran of at least one hundred snake catching incidents, he was keen to show off these skills to his closest neighbour.

"Barb, it's okay. I'll get my gear together and I'll be there soon."

"I'm sorry to be such an alarmist. Should be used to snakes around the farm, but not in my bloody great shed," she chortled, "Scared me half to death when I saw this bloody great big brown snake come out from under my tractor."

"How big was it, mate?"

There was a long pause before she answered, "I reckon it was about a good metre or more. I hope you're able to catch it safe. Don't get bitten, I mean."

Chook chuckled quietly, "I've been catching snakes for years. You know me. I'm a tough old bugger. Anyway, sit tight and I'll see you in a bit."

His gnarled, shaking hand gently put down the phone receiver. He glanced around the kitchen floor, looking for his snake catching gear. He found the reptile sack and the long snake hook discarded in a corner of the room. The snake catching jobs were few and far between. Fortunately, Barb was his next-door neighbour. His ute had broken down the other week and was at the nearest garage being fixed.

Picking up the gear, he slammed the kitchen door shut behind him and started the twenty-minute brisk walk in his bare feet to their shared fence line. In public, he wore his well-worn boots but around the farm, he didn't care. He was used to walking in bare feet. He was whistling to himself and grinning ear to ear. He was finally going to prove himself useful to Barb Hillman whom he had secretly loved since she had arrived in the district over thirty years ago.

He well remembered her arrival all those years ago. She had turned up one hot summer's day. She had towed her parents old caravan to the roadhouse, driving a battered old Ford Falcon. Mabel at the Batty had very kindly allowed her to stay camped there. Back then, Barb was a young twenty-something, with striking long brown hair and she lived in tight jeans and rock n roll t-shirts. Chook had struck up a friendship with the newcomer, but it wasn't long before another local Ryan Wayne Parsons appeared on the scene. Ryan had just lost his job as the Park Ranger and his family's farm as well. Their eyes locked together at the Roadhouse and that was pretty much it. Barb and Ryan became inseparable and when they got his farm back, they were rarely seen away from it. Chook disappeared into the background until Ryan died. But his advanced age still did not deter his thoughts of being romantically involved with Barb Hillman. He still hoped he could make the leap from friend to lover.

He reached the fence line and found the section where one strand of barbed wire was down. He carefully climbed over it and made his way through the dense underbrush. Barb's old, galvanised tractor shed soon came into view and he saw her leaning against her work ute. He had never seen her smoke openly before, but she was puffing away on a cigarette. When Barb saw his approach, she hastily tossed it to the ground and squashed it out with the heel of her work boot.

She looked guilty about it.

"Howdy," she greeted him, flashing her tight-lipped smile.

"I'm ready to go. Snake's still in there?"

She tipped her Akubra hat slightly over her left eye, studying him with her right, "Sure, Chook, it's still there. Likes my bloody work tractor too much."

Chook balanced his snake catching hook in one hand and dragged the sack across the hard ground in his other, "Stay here. I'll sort it."

He shoved open one of the large, shed doors and disappeared inside. His head was immediately trained on movement under her tractor. It didn't take long before he saw a long sleek brown body slithering and weaving its way over the straw around the tractor wheels.

He slowly took a step back and took a deep breath. He stepped forward and braced himself for a short fight with the snake. He angled the hook under its shiny head and pressed it head down against the ground. It's body and tail slashed wildly about, and Chook bravely came closer and positioned the opening of the sack over the reptile's head. The reptile completely disappeared headfirst into the hessian sack and Chook made quick work tying the string tight.

Glowing with a sense of pride, he walked out of the shed holding the sack up high in triumph.

"I got him for you."

"What are you going to do with him?"

Chook scratched his grey stubbled chin and replied, "I'll take him back home and later on, I'll drive far away and release him back into the bush. As a rule, I don't kill the snakes I get."

Barb inclined her head and lifted herself off the ute, "As long as it doesn't come back. Thanks for doing that. How much I owe you?"

"For you, it's on the house."

"Catch you later then," she winked at him and walked off, sticking her hands into the pockets of her work jeans.

Old Chook headed home, walking on air. He finally felt that he had been noticed.

He entered the back door into his kitchen and without as much as a second thought, he tossed the hessian sack with the snake withering inside it, into a corner. He whistled again as he started making himself a cup of tea.

The water on the stove came to boiling point and he splashed it into a mug. He sat down at his kitchen table which was full of old papers and brochures. He sipped from the mug and his hearing not being great, he failed to notice the slight creak of the kitchen door on its hinges.

His back was turned to the back door and the stove. Something hard connected with the top of his head and everything went black.

Sometime later, Old Chook opened his left eye a crack. He could see the ceiling looming large above him. He felt lightheaded and he knew he was lying stretched out on his hard kitchen floor. He didn't know how long he had been lying there for. The top of his head felt sore.

He wriggled his fingers and toes. He couldn't hear any sounds around him, except for the annoying loud ticking of the wall clock. He hoped it was safe to get up. He quietly lay there for another minute. His eyes darted side to side, taking in his surroundings. Nothing seemed to have changed around him. He noticed that the back door and the door leading to the loungeroom were both firmly closed. He couldn't recall closing either one of them. He appeared to be alone in his kitchen and he still didn't know what had happened to him.

He quickly moved to prop himself up on his bony left elbow, and before he had a chance to react, he saw a brown flash lunge at his face. It hissed at him and stuck his face several times more. He cried out in terror, not knowing what was happening. When his eyes finally could focus again, he found he was looking directly into the black angry eyes of the brown snake he had captured earlier. Somehow it had slipped out of the hessian bag and he noticed blood on its tail tip like someone had hacked at it. He could not recall injuring the snake, but it explained the vicious attack.

Chook crawled slowly out of its strike reach and when he was far enough, he gripped the edge of the kitchen table and pulled himself up. He realised that he didn't have much time before the deadly venom would take effect. His right hand picked up his phone receiver from its cradle. There was no dial tone. He followed the phone line and glancing at the wall plug, he saw that it had dislodged. The problem was that the brown snake was coiled right in front of it. It was poised to strike out again at the sign of any movement.

Chook's breathing started to labour after a few minutes, and he felt weakness in his body coming on. He could make it to the back door and safely out, but to walk to the main road was a good thirty minutes. To get to Barb's property, it was twenty minutes at a brisk walk. It really didn't matter which direction he took outside. He was a walking dead man either way.

He slumped down onto the floor and lay his head back. He was at least happy that he had his dentures in. A solitary tear trickled down his right cheek to his ear. He had decided not to fight death when it rapidly came to embrace him.

The brown snake slithered over his body and roved around the farm kitchen for the next twenty-four hours until discovered by a neighbouring farmer.

****

Duncan received the call announcing Old Chook's demise at nine o'clock in the morning. He was settled in his caravan bed after an early morning jog through the park, with Kimberley nestled comfortably into the crook of his left arm. He put his mobile phone down onto the floor and lay his head back on the pillow.

"I know," she said quietly, breaking seconds of silence, "You have to go and work. And I shouldn't be around here, with you."

"No."

He brushed his fingertips over her pale, ample breasts to her bare torso. And then brushed them over her full curvy hip. She smiled at him so sweetly which made it difficult for him to let her go.

"I mean yes. Look, my love. Just go and stay at my house. It's safer and Raquel's gone. The front door keys are under the pot plant at the back door. I'll see you later tonight."

"You promise?"

"I promise."

He kissed the top of her forehead and leapt out of bed. He was dressed in five minutes, in his conservative best. He didn't have time to shave and talked himself into believing that he didn't present too rough to face the world.

He went to briefly investigate Chook's farmhouse, studied the tragic scene carefully and spoke to Forensics who were there busy recording evidence.

Finally, he drove to Brumby Flat, and headed to the local police station. Soon after he had arrived, he immediately installed himself in the main office, opening his laptop. He tackled a few emails and then stopped.

Duncan rocked back and forth on the desk chair in the local police station. His fingers were raised in a steeple on his stomach. He had passed Constable Steve Willaston earlier, who had glared at him with his hooded hazel eyes. No word was exchanged between them, and Phil Duncan now sensed the depth of his own betrayal. It had started to concern him, but it was too late to repair the damage he had already done.

He turned his head towards the door when he heard Rich enter the office. He was smartly dressed in his navy suit, but Duncan noted that his white shirt was a bit soiled, like he had slept in it. With his arrival, Duncan could also smell a strong whiff of cigarette smoke in the air, which he had a disdain for.

As far as Duncan knew, Rich had spent the best part of the previous day interviewing locals, including Bill Goodall. The ex-ranger had little to say and Rich walked away with his questions unanswered. So, Rich went next door to Barb Hillman's property. He had hoped to get some more cooperation from her but all she revealed was her suspicions about Goodall.

In the end, Barb had turned her back to him and said in her abrupt manner, "If you want more information, detective, I might be persuaded with some pillow talk."

Rich was not sure if she was joking but thought about her words a bit. Then he had shrugged his shoulders and followed her back to her farmhouse. He spent the night there and had accidently left his tie behind on her dresser. His good white shirt was soiled as her bedroom floor was dusty and dotted with traces of dirt from her work boots. He forgot to question her and although he was only weeks out from retirement, he was not about to hasten it by telling Duncan who he had actually spent the night with.

Rubbing his now stubbly, unshaven chin, Rich said, "I came over as quick as I could. A snake bite, was it? Poor old Chook."

Duncan removed his glasses, rubbed his eyes and shook his head, "Yes but no. I think there's more to it. I don't think this is a straight-out accident. I had a good look around when I was there, at the farm."

"Right. Well. The bodies are piling up."

His partner smirked, "Yes, unfortunately they are. What happened to Old Chook is a stretch of the truth. I believe his was a cruel, calculated, cold blooded murder."

Rich crossed his arms and leaned back against the desk opposite. "Wow. You got some proof?"

"Not really. Not yet. But carefully consider all this information I'm about to unload and please, indulge me," Duncan took a deep breath and continued, "On face value, it looks like a brown snake got into Chook's house. And it happens in the country, and there's a sack found in the kitchen. He was probably trying to catch the snake. The doors in the kitchen are all closed. It's an accident. It makes sense to think that way, right?"

Rich inclined his head in agreement.

"But then, the snake catcher's hook is found outside, in the yard. Then there's this bump on Chook's head. Maybe he hit his head on something, like the table, getting away from the brown snake. But I don't think so. The more I think about it, it was staged to look like an unfortunate accident."

"Okay."

"I think Old Chook was either asked to go catch a snake for someone. Or else someone brought it direct to him, to his farmhouse. He was struck on the back of the head and left for dead. Forensics are working around the clock, so I am hoping they find some evidence to support my murder theory."

His partner sighed and flicked his eyes to the station ceiling.

"By Christ, I hope it's not another goddamn murder," he said, "I'm supposed to be retiring in sixty-five days from now. At the rate this investigation is going and the body count, I'll be working well past Christmas. Can't do it, mate."

"It can't be helped. It is what it is, Rich. By the way, Chook's real name is Charles James something. It sounded a bit posh. I guess calling himself Chook was easier."

"But why would anyone want the old fella dead? He just seemed to be a harmless old guy. A happy soul."

"I've thought about that. He was a bit of a talker. Old Chook knew lots of stories and local history. Maybe he knew just one story too many. One story best forgotten."

"You want me to interview the locals again?"

"Yeah, we'll start with Barb Hillman maybe and that other park ranger guy, Bill Goodall. And I'm going to go ahead and order Chook's phone records. We'll see who called him last."

Rich nodded his head and hitched up his trousers to his pot belly, "Okay. I'll approach Barb, I guess."

He turned to leave but then spun around, remembering to pass on information.

"By the way, mate. The tv and newspaper reporters are all around the Batty today, trying to get a story. But Banks is saying nothing and I'm not talking. Just a heads up, buddy."

Chapter Fourteen

Raquel admired her reflection in the bathroom mirror. She had just finished her make up for the job interview at the Batty Roadhouse. She was ready four hours ahead of time, but she was not the type to be late for a job interview anyway. She prided herself on her punctuality.

She dragged her mascara brush upward with one more flourish to her eyelashes and stood back from the mirror. Satisfied, she straightened her pale blue suit. Her blonde hair was trimmed back to shoulder length which framed her oval face perfectly.

She walked into her kitchen and flicked the electric kettle on. As she waited for it to boil, she opened the day's newspaper to read about the latest controversy surrounding Beecham's Bridge. There was a lot of media coverage about the recent ill-fated Folk Festival. She had heard about the accidental death of the lead singer, the lost Latvian mountain rescue team who reappeared in the festival crowd and the murdered roadhouse couple. As much as she told herself that she had no regard for Detective Phillip Duncan, she was still invested in his investigations. She was looking forward to reading any latest developments.

She opened to page three, and the headline leaped out at her immediately. She had to stop and read the article.

'Orgy Tragedy Claims Adelaide Family Man.'

"Oh, my god," she exclaimed aloud.

She read the first sentence over and over again, she couldn't believe that her ex-lover Ricardo was dead. Tears wildly streamed down her cheeks, splashed into her cleavage and ruined her flawless make up. She racheted to the bathroom after having a good cry to start the grooming process all over again.

She studied her reflection, noting her red rimmed hazel eyes. She grabbed a clean hand towel and wetting it slightly, she wiped her make up smeared face clean. She started to sob. The fact that Ricardo had been married and had left his family behind to grieve was not lost on her either. She felt guilt over their past sexual dalliances and upset that she would be his secret taken to the grave.

It took another five minutes to find her composure. Then she started to add a light foundation to start the make up process all over again.

It was well over an hour later before she was ready to face the world and leave for her job interview.

For a second time, she stood before the full-length mirror, straightening her matching jacket and skirt. She glanced down at her watch and grabbed her leather satchel bag from her kitchen stool. She walked out her front door in the main street and into a mild, sunny spring day.

She had her car already parked outside, waiting to go. As she fumbled for her car keys, she heard a woman's voice call out her name.

She turned sharply in the direction as the voice was not one familiar to her.

She saw a younger woman walking rapidly towards her, with auburn shoulder length hair, dressed in a smart aqua wrap dress. She was teetering on a pair of shiny emerald green pumps. As she came closer, Raquel recognised the pale blue-green eyes and the pouty ruby red hued lips.

They stopped on the asphalt road and stood still for a moment, each silently admiring their rivals' dress sense. For Raquel, it was a strange moment of déjà vu.

"Hey, wait. I'm so glad I found you," Geena Henderson exclaimed, having finally reached her, patting her pale freckled chest. She was slightly out of breath.

"What do you want? I thought my last message to you was pretty clear."

"Yes, I know. It was. But I was hoping…I'll just come out and say it, I guess. But I heard that Detective Duncan ingloriously dumped you."

Raquel glared at her, "Wow, news gets around fast," she snapped.

"It is a small town. Of course, I've moved into Brumby Flat and it was the first thing they all told me. It was like a crime had been committed."

"You've come here to gloat, have you? Is that what you want to do?"

"No, no," Geena vehemently shook her head, "I don't know anyone else here. I thought we might be friends. We do…well, we did share one thing in common," her voice nervously trailed off.

"Us? Friends? You must be crazy. I mean, out of your mind crazy. I don't want your kind of friendship. You can't be trusted."

Raquel turned her head away and grabbed her car door handle.

"Wait. Wait. We also have something else in common now."

She reluctantly turned her head back to look at Geena, her left eyebrow raised.

Geena continued, "We do. My husband and I have separated. That's why I'm here. Detective Duncan's fault totally. And he never call me. You were so right."

"I have no sympathy to show you."

"I am not asking for your sympathy. I am new here. I am asking for your friendship and your forgiveness. That's all I want."

Raquel sighed and looked back to her car, "Look, Geena. I've really got to go. Here's what I'll do. I'll think about it. I'll let you know. It's a bit of a shock to the system."

"Yeah. I understand."

She climbed into her Pontiac and drove off, with Geena still standing in the street watching her go.

When she had made enough distance, she relaxed her shoulders and put on the radio. She had a long fifty-kilometre drive to Beecham's Bridge before her and the last thing she had anticipated was bumping into Duncan's notorious one-night stand. The wrecker of her best friends' marriage.

As she drove down the country road, she went through a possible series of interview questions in her head.

When she arrived at the Batty Roadhouse, she was surprised to see the size of it and the unusual upside-down bat statue next to it. She parked her car near the front door.

She took a deep breath before she walked with a confident stride through the sliding glass doors.

Banksia Peterson peered around the kitchen wall when she heard the motion of the doors. She turned off the burners where she had been cooking up chicken patties for the brisk lunch trade. She brushed her hands over her soiled apron and hurried out to meet the stranger.

Raquel smiled at her, taking in Banksia's plain facial features and serious business demeanour. Her brown hair was done up in her usual no-nonsense top knot on her head. She stood only a fraction shorter than Raquel but she was the one wearing high heels. She imagined Banksia was wearing sensible shoes.

Raquel stretched out her hand over the counter to warmly shake Banksia's plump fleshy one.

"Hello. I'm Raquel Willaston. Lovely to meet you."

The proprietor's eyes lit up and she beamed, "Oh right. You're here for the interview. You're a bit early."

"I always like to be early. I hope it's okay."

"Of course. I've turned off the cooking anyway. We can talk at the table over there. You can call me Banks, by the way."

Raquel followed her, with the satchel tucked securely under her left arm.

As they sat down, she placed the satchel flat on the table to open it, but Banksia waved her hand.

"It's okay. I don't need to see anything else. Your resume and references were more than enough. All I really need to know is if you can fit this position. There is a lot to it. It's seven days a week. Long hours.

"Yes, so you said in your ad."

"I am up at the crack of dawn. I open at seven and I close at ten in the evening sometimes. Depends on the last customer in the bar."

"Oh, wow."

She leaned forward and bent over a finger one at a time as she continued, "You are a cook, a cleaner, a customer service professional, you manage the three motel rooms at the back and then you operate the weight bridge. I've run out of fingers," she said, giggling. "There's the mail to sort, but locals come in for that. You also have to manage the bar after hours. It's usually beers on Friday and Saturday nights. I end up closing earlier the other nights so it's not too bad."

"What time do you usually close for the night, Banks?"

"About nine. Usually. Except Fridays and Saturdays."

"So, it is best to live on the premises to run it."

Banksia nodded, "I can show you the living quarters later. It's a large bedroom with an ensuite, just behind the kitchen. There's no living area but basically you have the run of the roadhouse kitchen and dining room to yourself after hours."

Raquel straightened in her chair, taking it all in, "Well, that's good to know."

"What do you think? Would this arrangement suit you? I won't be leaving the Batty right away. I can still be here, training you for a couple of months."

Raquel looked around the interior. She was quiet for a minute, thinking.

Suddenly, a road train pulled up outside at the diesel pumps and Banksia rose from her chair. She dusted the front of her apron and pulled down her black t-shirt.

"I'll just serve them and come back to you," she said, before heading to the shop counter in readiness to work the till.

While she was busy for the next ten minutes, Raquel had time to glance around the roadhouse and familiarise herself with the set up. She noted the two rows of shelves stacked with a selection of staple groceries for locals and the shelf by the counter filled with chocolates and other confectionary. She counted the tables in the dining area and scanned the well-stocked bar to the far right of the premises. It seemed to be well laid out with security cameras in place.

When Banksia returned to the table, she asked her, "Where would you be staying? That's if you are training me."

"Easy. I can stay in a motel room. They aren't frequently in use."

"What about the security aspect?"

"Oh. I have the cameras on twenty-four hours. During the day, the park ranger is around. Sullivan O'Grady."

Raquel blinked hard, "Oh, my god. Sullivan's here too?"

"You know him, do you?"

"Oh, yes. Used to come into the Raindrops Shop for his coffee. He's a real nice guy."

"That's right," Banksia exclaimed, "You live in Brumby Flat. Then you would know Detective Phil Duncan too."

"Oh yeah, I certainly do know him," Raquel snorted, fully prepared to give Banksia her unrestrained opinion of Duncan.

She stopped in mid breath when Banks nodded her head enthusiastically, "Isn't he a lovely man? He and his partner have been so kind to me over the loss of my parents."

Raquel then realised it was not a good idea to vent. Instead, she watched a large blowfly climb the wall beside the proprietor's ear.

"Yes, very nice guy. He's helped me too, for sure."

"You've lost someone?"

"Yes. His wife was my best friend."

Her deep-set brown eyes softened and she reached over and squeezed Raquel's hand, "I'm sorry. Well, I've made up my mind. No more interviews. I think you're perfect to run the Batty for me. If you'll accept the challenge of course."

Raquel smiled and as she was about to give her an answer, a mobile phone rang out.

Banksia reached into her apron pocket, "Sorry about this. I might have to take this. Hello? The Batty."

She listened intently and fiddled with a stray strand of hair as she did.

Finally, she said, "Okay. I'll see if I can get the message to him."

She ended the call and lay the phone on the tabletop, "Oh, no. Apparently no one can reach Detective Duncan. His girlfriend injured herself at training today. She's a firefighter you know."

"Nothing serious, I hope. It's Kimberley, right?"

"Yeah. They said she's in hospital but she's okay. They've been trying Detective Duncan's mobile, but it seems to be switched off. He's not answering."

"That doesn't sound right to me," Raquel added her two cents.

Banksia picked up her mobile again and tried Duncan's number herself. The call went straight to his messages and she placed it back onto the table.

"That is strange."

"Banks, I accept the job. Thanks very much."

"Great. You'll love working here."

Suddenly, a loud sound completely unrelated to the national park and the farmland surrounds rang out. A huge flock of galahs, a shock of pink and white, took flight from a nearby gumtree and streaked across the brilliant blue sky. They watched the colourful display in awe as the chattering birds flew past the panoramic front windows of the Batty Roadhouse.

Banksia widened her eyes, "Did you hear that? It sounded like a gunshot. Do you think it was?"

Raquel got up and turned to leave, "Banksia. Can you please tell me where Phil Duncan is? I'll go find him and tell him about his girlfriend."

"Are you sure?"

"Yeah. You should call the police maybe. It did sound like a shot being fired."

Banksia bit down on her bottom lip. She studied Raquel's eyes hard before telling her what their plans were, "I think the detectives said they were going to see Barb Hillman. She owns the farm across the highway. You take the first left turn. Her gates at the end of the dirt track."

"Thanks. Talk to you soon."

Another shot rang out and it was enough to make her sprint out to her car. Raquel had no idea what she should do if there was trouble. However, she knew she could not stand by and let Duncan face danger alone.

Chapter Fifteen

Duncan had agreed with Rich who was interviewing who, and Duncan said he would see former park ranger Bill Goodall first and then catch up with his partner at Barb Hillman's property after. Rich had interviewed Goodall before but not much had been achieved that time. Bill had kept all his cards close to his big broad chest.

Duncan's aging white station wagon wasn't exactly made for rural dirt roads, but he pushed it uphill on Beecham's Drive. The tyres caught in some wet sand in a few patches. Somehow, Duncan managed to steer his car out of trouble.

He found the gates with yellow painted tyres either side and drove through. It was a meandering, pot-holed, narrow trail to reach Goodall's modest farmhouse. It was a plain transportable home with a wide full-length veranda.

Duncan parked on an incline next to the work shed and brushed his hands over his shirt cuffs and then tucked his shirt back into his fawn-coloured trousers. Climbing onto the veranda, he knocked soundly on the front door. There was no answer. He knocked again, louder this time.

He scanned his eyes over the landscape from his position on the veranda and caught a movement.

Bill Goodall waved to him from the tree line and had started to walk briskly in the direction of the farmhouse. He was carrying a pair of pliers in his beefy right hand, so Duncan assumed he had been busy mending property fences.

Bill was a tall, broad barrel of a man. Standing at six foot four, he towered over most people, including Phil Duncan. He was the type of man you would think twice to taunt. His curly grey hair was tinged with red, and his full beard was still an orange red, befitting of his Scottish heritage.

"Hey, you're the other detective?" He said, wiping his soiled broad hands on his denim overalls, "More questions, is it?"

Duncan nodded, his facial expression solemn, "I don't know if you're aware of it yet, but Old Chook's dead."

Bill's face turned ashen grey, "Yeah, I heard about it. Banks told me this morning. She said he died from a snake bite. A big brownie."

"That's really why I'm here."

"Would you like a cuppa? Just going to make some tea for myself."

"I'm not usually a tea drinker, but I'd love some today."

Bill barrelled his way through his front door. He gestured with his broad hand for Duncan to take up a stool at the island bench in his neat kitchen. He popped the kettle on the electric stove. They had to wait ten minutes for the water to boil and no one spoke during that time. While Duncan patiently waited, he had a good hard look over Bill's kitchen. He noticed various tools strewn across the island bench and a shotgun propped up in a dark corner.

Duncan sat there with his hands clasped together and smiled as Bill passed him the mug of piping hot tea as promised.

"Earl Grey," he said, lifting his own cup.

"Thanks."

As Bill settled his bulk into the stool opposite, blocking sunlight from the kitchen window, he remarked, "Foxes."

"Pardon me?"

"My gun's over there. I use it to kill foxes around my property. They go after my chickens."

"Right."

"I don't know why I'm a person of interest to you guys."

Duncan smirked.

"Well, I guess there's not too many people left who were around here, from over thirty years ago. It is a cold case but now that we've had some recent murders, maybe this killer is still very much alive today. Killing local people to keep their past deeds quiet."

Bill rubbed his red tinged beard, "I liked Old Chook. He was a good mate to lots of people around Beecham's Bridge. I can't believe he's gone out that way. He was an experienced snake catcher. We all used him, when we needed him. But I think you should be talking to Barb Hillman. She is a firecracker and a ball breaker, that one."

"You don't trust her?"

"Nah. I never have, mate. She's only got one agenda. To look after herself. She was friends with my wife, you know. She put a wedge between us. My wife went off and left me and the farm a couple of years ago."

"What happened?"

"I haven't talked about this in years. Don't know if I rightly can..." his voice trailed off and he stared hard at a kitchen wall.

"You started this, so you can't stop now. You can't tell me it was nothing."

"Yeah, okay. Barb's a cunning fox. She's cute or she's this cruel bitch. She actually told my wife, to her face, that I was having an affair with her. My wife believed every word she said and she up and left me. But I did make the mistake of telling my wife once that I had dated Barb just before she met her lover boy. Of course, Barb was a stunner and a head turner when she was much younger."

"I see. Were you dating her when you were the park ranger?"

Bill arched a bushy eyebrow and nodded, "Yeah, I think so. I remember picking her up for this one date we had. She was living in her caravan at the Batty. The old lady who ran it, well, she had a soft spot for the girl. Let her park the van around the back of the Batty and stay there. Free of charge."

"She wasn't living with that Parsons fellow?"

"That mad bastard? Oh no. He turned up later. Anyway, I took young Barb on a picnic in the park. We ate lunch by this nice waterhole. Tried my moves on her but she was a bit high and mighty. Our date was short, and I dropped her back at her van. A few days later, next I saw her in the Batty dining room, looking into Ryan Wayne Parson's mean eyes. They were holding hands like they were an item. They were all lovey-dovey like. It made my stomach churn watching them carrying on. Ryan was sort of a mate of mine too, but as soon as I saw the two of them together, I moved on. Had enough of it."

"Okay."

"It was strange, detective," he added with a wistful sigh.

"What was strange?"

"How she came into big money so sudden like," he continued, taking another gulp of tea, "Ryan lost his family farm to the bank. He had lots of defaults. His family had owned their land for a couple of generations. I nearly felt sorry for that poor mean bastard. Anyway, young Barb Hillman turned up to Beecham's Bridge. Not a bloody dime to her name as I remember it. Good old Mabel let her buy food and coke on credit. Then six weeks later, they pay cash to get his farm back from the bank. Maybe her old lady or old man died. Who knows? It's a mystery where all this cash suddenly came from."

He stopped and took a big gulp of tea.

"Old Chookie had a theory though. He recently talked to me about it. Confided in me. He told me not to say anything to Barb, or anyone else in fact. But I think it's best to tell you."

Duncan leaned in, finally fishing out his small notebook from his back pocket.

"Where did he think the money came from?"

"Sorry, I forgot he had two theories. First, he thought maybe old Mabel had lent the money to Barb. She was a real honey. Or else, they stole the money from someone. Chook said Ryan probably did that all on his own. Chook said Barb would be an innocent party."

Bill proceeded to tell all. He didn't withhold any information from Duncan.

"Ryan was a park ranger for a bit. You already know that. He carried his shotgun with him, and he'd fire it off in the park. Terrified a lot of tourists. Lots of complaints reached the department so they had to let him go."

He paused for a moment, deep in thought.

"Yeah, I remember that Chook even said Ryan quite possibly killed that young couple from over thirty years ago. To keep the money source hush-hush. Probably thought no one would miss them or find their graves out in the scrub."

Duncan nodded, "Well. A pity Ryan Wayne Parsons' dead. Can't ask him."

"Barb's not."

Duncan closed his notebook after writing a flurry of words. He rose from the stool and stretched his back.

"Thank you for your cooperation today. And the tea as well."

Bill inclined his head, "Happy to help, detective. But can I ask you something?"

"Sure. Go for it."

"Was it an accident? What happened to Old Chook?"

"It's still under investigation. That's all I can say about it."

Duncan turned and the screen door squealed and swung on its hinges as he left.

He raced down the veranda steps to his car. As he opened the driver's side door, he realised he still had more questions than answers. Parsons was dead and people were still being snuffed out.

Suddenly, the phone call came for which he had been anxiously waiting.

"Hello, Senior Detective Duncan."

He listened intently before thanking the caller.

He stared at the hard ground for a moment and then, auto dialled Rich's mobile.

"Hey, mate. I know who spoke to Chook last. They said it *was* Barb Hillman. I'll meet you at her place as soon as I can. She must know something."

He started his car and made an awkward U-turn over some protruding tree roots, which were all that remained of a tree which had been lopped down to the end of its stump. He followed the rough trail back to the dirt road and as he followed it back towards the main highway, he remembered he had to swing right onto the next dirt road to find his way to Barb's farm.

He cruised over the unmade road at eighty kilometres an hour, sending plumes of bulldust flying but forgot to slow down to take the next sharp corner. The back of his car slid sideways, with dirt and dust flying and Duncan was forced to apply the brakes harder than he intended.

Suddenly, the car stopped careening forward and the jolt winded him for a brief moment. The engine was still running, and he felt the wheels spinning wildly underneath. He frowned and realised that his wheels were firmly stuck in a vast patch of mud in the middle of the road.

He cursed loudly and got out of the car, surveying the damage. The front bumper was cracked and hanging down and a tyre had popped. He kicked the tyre and let go a few choice swear words.

He calculated the distance to Barb's farm. He was sure that it was just over the crest of the next hill and determined that the start of her property boundary was about a twenty-minute walk south along the adjacent dirt road. He carefully stepped away from his bogged vehicle, trying to avoid getting mud on his new leather shoes. He was not too successful and as he walked on, he had to stand momentarily on the grass verge, scraping it off. He locked the car and started to trudge his way up the hill.

The Last Shot

Barb Hillman was whistling a well-known country and western tune as she stood on top of her work truck, restacking hay bales for the cattle in the back paddock. She stopped for a moment to brush some long hay strands off her grubby western check shirt when she saw the older city detective Rich heading up her dirt and gravel driveway. She then dusted her hands over her jeans and knitted her eyebrows under her battered hat.

He was dressed as always in his suit, with a white shirt tucked over his blue trousers to hide his pronounced beer gut. He lifted his right hand and gestured a hello.

Barb sighed heavily and flipped her long grey hair in its ponytail, off her shoulder. She rubbed her blunt tipped nose and said a quiet hello when he was within hearing range.

"Well, what can I do for you, old fella?" She effortlessly jumped down from the tray and casually picked up her trusty shotgun which was leaning against the truck driver's door.

"Hey, well, got more questions for you, Barb. About your old mate, Chook."

"Again? Look, I don't know what more to say to you guys."

She turned her back to him and started to stride towards the edge of the paddock, intent on checking the water level in the cattle trough. The shotgun was swinging against her side as she walked at a brisk pace.

Rich followed her, "I know it's hard to lose a good friend, a good mate, but the killer needs to be brought in to face justice. If he called you that day—"

She cut him off mid-sentence, "I told you guys before. Chook didn't tell me anything new under the sun. He didn't bloody call me. I didn't see him the last two days he was alive. Okay? This convo's done with. Now, if you don't mind, I've got a shitload of work to do. I really do. Animals to feed."

Rich put his hand on his hips and his eyes squinted under the harsh glare of the day. She was standing conveniently with her back to the sun, having reached the water trough and a cluster of gumtrees. He then leaned casually against the trunk of an old, twisted blue gum, hands in trouser pockets.

"Look. I know you're frustrated about going over old ground again, but you should be concerned. A bit nervous. In the last few weeks, people have been dropping dead like flies around here. Actually, that's Detective Duncan's expression I'm using. Not really mine."

She kept her back turned to him and said quietly, "I can't help you, detective."

"You know, Barb. I have this theory. I think you know a lot more than you're saying. You've lived in the district a long, long time. Come on, Lovey. You have to have seen things, heard something."

She didn't answer him. She had second thoughts about checking the water trough and turned to walk back to her parked truck.

"You shared this property with an old boyfriend way back. You have to know something."

She kept walking fast, her back facing him.

Not to be deterred, he continued talking to her retreating back, "And I don't understand why you can't tell us what else you know. You could be helping a lot of people here. Do you remember anything? Anything at all?"

Getting no reaction from her, Rich tried another tact. By telling a recent truth.

"The phone records came back. We know where the last call came from. You called Chook last. We know that you spoke to him on the phone. Before he died."

She stood next to her truck and leaned against the drivers' door. She inclined her head and when she finally looked up directly at him, her eyes had narrowed to slits.

Through gritted teeth, she said in a low snarly voice, "I told you no. I'm not saying anything. Because I don't want some kind of kangaroo court chasing me down."

Barb Hillman took up her shotgun in a fluid, well-practised motion and the bullet she released hit Rich square through his torso. She never blinked her eyes as she pulled the trigger. A thin curl of smoke followed from the gun barrel. She dropped the gun down, pointing it to the ground. She turned her head away, started to walk off, the gun balanced in her right hand, and she left him on his back, gasping for each breath.

Duncan who had just arrived on Barb's property, heard the gunshot ring out like a clap of thunder from his position near the line of trees on the opposite end of the paddock. He was standing exposed, out in the open. He ran flat out for the nearest large gumtree for cover. A bullet just missed him, he even felt the rush of air as it flew in front of his face, splintering a patch of wood on the tree truck beside him. He made it safely as another bullet whizzed by. He grabbed his handgun from underneath his shirt. He didn't know what was going on and who was firing, but he knew well enough to know that he was in trouble and more than likely, facing the danger alone. He didn't know where his partner was. He texted frantically away on his mobile phone, but no return message came back. He knelt down, his back against the tree trunk and tried to level his erratic breathing. He had never been involved in a shootout before and his mind was racing with overwhelming thoughts of dying, of being killed. However, there were no more shots being fired around him.

He finally leaned over and looked around the tree trunk cautiously. When his eyes had adjusted to the bright midday sunlight, he saw the back of a lone figure running towards Barb Hillman's farmhouse shed. He waited several minutes to ensure it was reasonably safe to emerge from his cover.

Staying as low to the ground as he could manage it, Duncan raced briskly to the next tree, his gun raised. He realised he would have to risk being out in the open air if he wanted to follow the shooter to the farmhouse at the edge of the large paddock. He was visibly shaking. This was more than a threat he was faced with. He still couldn't see Rich, so he came to the conclusion that he had no real back up.

Before he took the risk to leave cover, he rang his unit.

"Hey, it's Duncan. We have a shooter up here near Beecham's National Park. I've had shots fired directly at my head but I'm okay."

He listened to his colleague then added in a low voice, "Yeah. I have lost sight of Rich. No response. I can't sit and wait for you. I need to find him."

He quickly gave directions to Barb Hillman's farm and closed the call. Half crouching, he swiftly crossed the open clearing, heading in the direction of another line of trees and underbrush. This time he made it safely, with no gunshots flying around him. He stepped behind a huge white gumtree and sighed heavily. He would have to wait for the back up to arrive.

Suddenly, he heard twigs snapping and he turned nervously, pointing his gun in the direction of the sounds. He saw Raquel Willaston emerge from behind the next tree. Her hazel eyes were wide as she looked at the gun barrel she was faced with. She relaxed when her eyes focused on Duncan.

"What the…Keep your bloody fool head down," he snapped at her, lowering his weapon. He then leaned forward, grabbed her hand roughly and pushed her face down to the ground. She wasn't happy about that, as she had her best white shirt and pale blue suit on.

He kept his handgun raised in the air, "What the fuck are you doing here? What possessed you? We're in the middle of a shootout."

"I didn't want to come here, but your girlfriend's at the hospital. She's okay, I think it's only minor, but I had to let you know. And then I heard gunfire."

"Keep your head down. How did you get here?"

"I parked at the gates and walked up. I heard shots, so I kept to the trees. Anyway, I have to go now. Done my duty."

He pushed her back down again, "You can't just walk in here and then go? This is a fuckin' shootout."

"Watch me. I plan to keep my head." She readied herself to retreat when she turned her head and added, "By the way, congratulate me. I just got the roadhouse job."

Hidden behind the tree trunk, she got up from the ground and dusted her knees off, when he reached out and grabbed her arm.

"Wait. Wait just a minute. Do you hear noises?"

She listened and heard the groaning too.

"Yeah, I think it's coming from over there."

"You stay here. Stay low. I'll investigate."

He slipped through the bushes and soon found Rich. He was lying with the back of his head resting against a gumtree trunk, his right hand clasping his stomach, where a spreading rash of red blood oozed out, over his jacket, across his shirt and onto the dry, leafy ground. He had dragged himself there, leaving a trail of blood for metres.

"Fuck," Duncan exclaimed, his eyes wide behind his glasses.

"She shot me. The bitch shot me. I thought she even liked me. Big mistake. What a bitch, hey?" Rich said in a raspy, laboured voice, trying to shift his position but Duncan clasped his other arm to hold him still.

"Hey, don't move mate. I'll call for an ambulance."

Rich rolled his head side to side, "Don't worry about it. They won't make it in time. I know what this means. It's not good. Not happy. I was ready to retire, you know."

Raquel appeared, having crawled her way through the same bushes, "It's okay. I'll call."

She dusted the dry dirt and leaves off her suit.

"Who is that?"

"Raquel Willaston. My wife's friend."

Rich managed to nod his head and smile at her.

Duncan searched Rich's pale face, "What do you need?"

"You got a light? I need a ciggie really bad."

"Sorry, mate. I don't smoke. She doesn't either."

"Oh shit. I'm really screwed then. Hey, mate. Get that bitch there for me, okay. Promise me you'll get her. Barb's a real loony tune. Be careful mate. She shot me like I was nothing. Like I was just a piece of piss."

Duncan looked up at Raquel with a pained, searching expression. She shook her head in response, her mobile pressed to her ear. She had already formed the opinion that Rich was a dying man. She could see he had lost a lot of blood and his eyes had started to lose life's lustre. But Duncan was struggling with the reality of the situation. He was trying not to think the worst.

"I'll get her, Rich. Bring her to justice."

Rich suddenly coughed up some blood, which spewed over his chin and shirt. He added in his weakened voice, "I think we've found the killer. Of your parents, the singer, the Petersons and perhaps more people. She's involved, for sure."

"Still, we need the proof."

Rich gripped Duncan's arm and now struggled to get his words out, "Mate, the proof is she's gone and fuckin' killed me too. And Chook."

"Don't talk like that. You'll be right. The ambulance is on its way."

Rich grinned and appeared paler than ever. He coughed up some blood again and said in a whisp of a voice, "Phil, I'm not going to make it. Give my love to my kids, okay. I know they loved their mother and I wasn't the best father by a mile."

He managed a few more words before his facial expression became frozen in time. His eyes glazed over as he stopped breathing. Duncan let go of a single tear which rolled down his right cheek while Raquel turned her head away and whispered quietly the only prayer that she knew.

He took up his gun firmly and spun on his heel, "Stay here. I'm not going to wait. I'm going after her."

She tried to reason with him. She rested her right hand on his shoulder, but he shook her hand away.

"Wait. And what are you hoping to achieve, Phil? Have you considered that maybe she's not working alone? You might get yourself killed, for god's sake."

"I can stop her escaping. I'm sure she'll make a run for it. Stay here with Rich."

"But the poor man's dead," she retorted, half whispering the fact.

"Yeah. Thanks to me. That's my fault. I sent him here to interview her."

"Phil, please. Don't leave me here. Don't do this all on your own."

Duncan lowered his head, said nothing in reply and started weaving his way steadily through the bushes and sparse undergrowth. A couple of kookaburras laughed overhead, somewhere high in the gumtrees.

When he reached the wood paling fence behind the shed, he rose very slowly, with gun poised and ready to fire. He ducked through a broken part of the timber railings and step by step, he approached the rear of the galvanised, rusty old tractor shed. He was trying to be quiet, but his shoes crunched down on the odd brittle dry patch of gum leaves and twigs. He sidled up to a back door which was slightly ajar. It was just wide enough to allow him to squeeze through, and he slipped inside, plunging into the depths of a horse box in shadow. He held his breath and listened out for a sound of any kind. Duncan exhaled quietly, and then drew another breath. He took a tentative step deeper into the stall. Still, he heard no sound within the shed. He wondered if Barb Hillman had already escaped. Or perhaps she had returned to her farmhouse to make a stand there.

He peered anxiously around the stall open door and slowly rose to his feet. His eyes had finally adjusted to the dim light. He held his gun to his chest, his fingers clutching it tight.

He took a tentative step forward and heard a footfall to his right. It crunched down on a raised bed of straw.

"Hey, detective, I got you right in my sights. Don't you bloody move a muscle."

She had effectively cornered him in the shed.

Duncan dropped his gun reluctantly to his side and shifted his gaze in her direction. Barb Hillman had her shotgun raised and pointed squarely at his head.

He realised that he had nowhere to go to save himself.

"The Spanish inquisition man himself. Well, well. You had to bloody poke your noses into my business, didn't you? No one asked me fuckin' questions until you and your detective mate damn well turned up at Beecham's Bridge," she barked at him.

He let his gun fall to the ground with a soft thud. He raised his hands slightly and said in a calm voice, "It's too late to make a run for it, Barb. What happens next, well, it's up to you. Better for you, if you lay down your weapon."

Her response showed in her screwed-up nose.

"Go fuck yourself, cop. You're my ticket out of here, don't you know?" She gave him a sly wink and continued, "Yeah. That's right, detective, I can use you as my hostage. We're gonna try that angle, okay? I'm sure they'll let me go, as long as I got you."

"You've got yourself quite the body count, Barb."

"If it makes you feel any better, I didn't know that hippie couple had a kid. My Ryan was a good man; he bought his farm for us with the money we took. I wasn't going to let you destroy his memory and drag it through the fuckin' mud that way."

"He killed…"

She cut him off, "He killed just once, he did it for us. To give us a future together."

Duncan smirked, "True. You accomplished so much on your own, being responsible for the murders of the Petersons who owned the roadhouse, Old Chook, now, Rich and the folk singer Hannah."

"That bloody diva? I had nothing to do with her," she snapped. "Don't pin that death on me, detective."

"Really?"

"You heard me. I didn't kill the singer, but you did forget one in your murder count. Your mother. Ryan let me finish her off. I did her a great kindness you know. She was badly damaged goods already. Ryan had already got stuck into her. I helped put her out of her misery."

Duncan took in a sharp breath and glared at her with hardened eyes.

"Yeah. The truth hurts, detective," she said smugly, "I understand. But it was hard to say goodbye to my old mate,

Chook. I'd known the old fella a long, long time. At least, I didn't have to watch him die."

"Then, you planted the brown snake?"

She nodded her head.

Suddenly, she heard a twig snap to her left side and Barb turned her head slightly, just enough to see Raquel nervously holding a handgun pointed in her direction.

"Christ. Who's this then? You bought some trumped up party girl with you? Is she here to protect you?" She chortled, still waving the loaded shotgun at Duncan, "Put it down, you silly dumb little fool."

Raquel fervently shook her head and cocked the trigger slowly, "No. You let him go. Now."

Duncan swallowed hard and realised that she had possession of Rich's police issued handgun.

"Raquel, please don't do this…"

"It's okay, Phil. I'm right," she replied back, her voice a little shaky but her hands seemed to be holding the handgun steady enough.

Barb brandished an evil, twisted smile, "You're making a bloody big mistake."

When she finished the sentence, Raquel lowered the pistol slightly and squeezed the trigger off rapidly. Her shot hit Barb just above her left kneecap and sent her screaming and falling onto her good right knee. She lost her control over her shotgun, which now pointed to the dusty ground. Duncan didn't think twice about it. He took his opportunity to rush forward and wrestled the shotgun out of her grasp. She grimaced with pain and was unable to fight him off. She was bent over, her lined face contorted in pain, cradling her bloodied leg.

He turned the shotgun barrel on her and backed away two paces. He had a clear shot if he needed to pop one off. Using his foot, he pushed his own discarded handgun well out of her reach.

Raquel lowered the gun which was still clutched hard in her hands, and she hopped back a couple of feet as well.

It was then that they all heard the approach of multiple police and ambulance sirens in the distance.

"Barbara Hillman, you're under arrest." He proceeded to read Barb her rights.

"Wow. That was a good shot you pulled off," he said, nodding his head to Raquel.

"Thanks, but you should be really thanking my son. He's been teaching me to shoot rabbits at the McCathy's place. Been good to let off some steam," she replied, adding with less enthusiasm, "Especially after what you did to me. Dumping me like yesterday's laundry. It's a good job I didn't shoot you by complete accident. Or I guess I could've let her do it for me. Kill you."

He raised an eyebrow and considered her last words. He didn't argue the point and just nodded his head frantically in her direction.

The End of the Story

A good two months had passed since the siege at Barb Hillman's farm. Detective Duncan, working from a tip-off provided by Banksia Peterson, drove back into the town of Brumby Flat. He wasn't heading home as much as he was on a mission to look up and briefly renew an old acquaintance. He cruised down the main street, passing the hardware store and the post office, then turned into the next side street on the left.

He slowed down, eyes squinting under his glasses. looking at the house numbers and finally parked his old white station wagon in front of number thirty-eight. The house itself was an old transportable one, badly in need of paint and repair. As he unfurled his tall, lithe frame from his car, the front screen door swung wide open on its creaky hinges.

Misty Rae Phoenix emerged, wearing her faithful pleated floral skirt teamed with a rainbow-coloured poncho she had purchased for a dollar from a local op shop. In her hand, she held a large water bottle. She smiled at him and pushed back her long, wild but meticulously braided hair with her free hand.

"Hi. I've been looking for you," he announced as he walked purposely forward, resting his hands on his hips.

Misty Rae glanced down at him, from her higher vantage point of the front timber porch, "Well. I think you didn't look hard enough. I've been here for about a month or two. It's a nice town. And I knew you had the hots for me, detective."

He grinned broadly, "I'm sure I never gave you *that* impression. Ever."

She flicked her eyelashes in a face weathered obviously by a life lived on the road and dependent on the generosity of strangers, "A real shame. I thought we had struck up a bit of a connection at the concert night. Backstage fireworks of our own."

After a few seconds, she started to laugh heartily and clapped her hands together, "Relax, detective. Just joking around with you."

"You must know why I'm really here to see you."

She shook her head. "No idea, detective. But you'd better move quick. I'm packing up my gear this afternoon and hitting the road again. Getting on the interstate bus in the morning. There's a massive music festival coming to Lismore and it's a way to go."

"Not happening. You'll have to put all your travel plans on hold, Misty Rae."

He had her immediate attention. She turned her head and studied his serious expression closely. He had lowered his tone so only she could hear him.

"Excuse me?"

"Misty Rae, I've come here to discuss the murder of Hannah Dee Wainwright with you. We have some unfinished business."

She flinched and took a long swig from her water bottle. Her brown eyes averted his intense blue stare.

"Hey. You're asking the wrong person. Anyway, I read in the papers that you've already found your killer. The end."

She turned to go back inside but Duncan joined her on the porch in one long stride, reached out and firmly gripped her left arm. She stopped in mid-step, the bracelets of bells around her ankles made an abrasive jingling sound.

"It took me awhile to piece it all together. Others will too. You had a perfect window of opportunity, and you took it. But still, I think to myself why you did it?"

"What? Are you arresting me?"

He relaxed his grip and let his hand fall away. "Well. If you admit to doing the deed, they may go easier on you. Right now, I'm really too tired to bother chasing you. I'm going to leave it entirely up to you. If you go ahead and leave Brumby Flat now, it will be a whole lot worse for you."

"I'm innocent. I didn't kill the bitch," she protested, but she didn't look up at him as she said the words. She cleared her throat nervously and took another gulp of water.

Duncan leapt down from the porch and straightened his pinstripe shirt.

"You did just call her a bitch. Anyway, that's your take on it. I know different," he remarked with a good dose of sarcasm, "It's only a matter of time before someone else figures it out. It's your choice. I'll leave you to make it."

He walked away and did not look back. He jumped back into his car and drove off. He had enough personally to deal with, and his conscience told him she would give herself up.

Maybe not today but possibly tomorrow.

He stopped his car as soon as he turned back into the main street. He picked up his mobile phone and automatically dialled a number he knew very well.

It took a few seconds before a familiar voice said hello.

He took a deep breath and spoke in his low deep voice which he knew she liked.

"Hello. It's me. I know it's been a little while."

He heard her audibly gasp on the other end. He didn't rush in to fill the empty space. He gave her some time to answer him.

"What do you want, Phillip Duncan?" Raquel replied, her voice low and terse.

"You're right to the point," he smirked.

"Yes."

"Kimberley is pregnant. I feel conflicted, just at the moment. Thought we might meet up and have a friendly old chat. Like we used to do."

She didn't reply as quickly as he had hoped.

Finally, she said, "Congratulations. But I'm not interested. You chose her and you let me go. I don't want to know about your screwed up feelings now. Don't bother me again in this lifetime, Phil Duncan."

"Wait," he said rapidly, "I have something else to say to you."

He heard her sigh heavily on the other end, "Go on then."

"I wanted to say thank you. I owe you my life that day."

"That's okay. Now please go away."

She closed the call.

****

Halfway through another warm autumn day and Raquel was starting to gather momentum at her new job at the Batty Roadhouse. Not being blessed with Banksia's good fortune,

Raquel had everything seeming to happen all at once. Bells, honks, cowbells and chimes went off at once at regular intervals. She usually had someone at the weighbridge, a family waiting for a big takeaway order and another lot wanting to check into the motel.

She had spent most of the day, trying to keep up with the ridiculous pace of it all. Finally, just past midday, she got a break. Just one of the local farmers appeared and had ordered himself a serve of fish and chips.

As the fat splattered away in the fryer, she lowered the basket of chips into it. Then she popped the batter-coated fish fillets into a separate basket and lowered it also into the splattering oil. As she did, she thought about the recent past. She was surprised how fast she had stopped crying over Phil Duncan. He had moved on with his new younger girlfriend and she was relieved that they had left town together. Last she had heard, they were living back in his Adelaide townhouse, making preparations for the arrival of their baby. Her son Steve was not taking the new situation so well, but she knew he needed more time to get over Kimberley.

She heard the front sliding glass doors open and shut but she didn't turn around this time. She was too busy concentrating on making the fish and chips perfectly crisp for her customer, a local farmer who was patiently waiting at a café table.

"I'll be with you in a minute," she cried out almost instinctively.

Then she heard the familiar voice she never imagined she would ever hear again in her lifetime.

"Howdy. Hey girlie, it's me. And I've come a hell of a long way to look for you."

She turned her head and accidentally dropped the basket of hot chips on the slate floor as she did. It clattered across the floor near her feet.

Phil Proctor stood in the doorway, slowly removing his white Stetson cowboy hat to reveal his mop of grey hair. His blue eyes crinkled gently at the corners as he grinned broadly at her. He looked a bit shy as well, not sure how she might react seeing him again. He nervously rolled the hat back and forth in both hands.

"It's been about nine or ten months, I reckon," he continued in his harsh whisper of a voice. He stopped fidgeting with his hat. He looped the forefinger of his right hand through his leather studded belt. He was wearing pale, stone washed skinny jeans which were so tight, they left nothing to the imagination. He oozed confidence in his own sex appeal.

Raquel said nothing, she stood there just staring back at him.

"Well, I guess I've really surprised you, ma'am. Shocked you even."

He stood there, waiting to see if she would react. He knew that if she came into his arms and if he ever held her there again, there would be no going back.

Finally, she said, "Yeah, you have."

Raquel let go of the basket of fish fillets and it fell back with an angry splash into the fat, and the hungry farmer looked on and moaned. He knew his fried lunch was at risk of never being prepared.

She wrestled desperately with the back ties of her apron, threw it to the ground angrily and raced around the front counter and ran straight into Proctor's arms. His good hat fell to the ground, but he didn't care about that.

He curled his strong, sinewy arms immediately around her and held her tight against his heaving chest. She heard his heart beating fast under his western check shirt. He tipped her chin up to reveal her face with the tears freely running down her cheeks to her lips. He gently wiped them away with the fingers of his free hand. He felt nothing but love and a strong desire for her.

"I ran away from you. Sweet Jesus, how I ran. As hard as I tried, I couldn't forget you, my sweetheart." He leaned in and kissed her lips with a mix of experienced tenderness and hot intensity which affirmed his mastery in the art of seduction. It was the thrilling and breath-taking kiss that she remembered quite well. The kiss lasted long enough to convince Raquel that he was indeed real again, holding her and standing right in front of her.

When they both finally resurfaced for air, she asked him straight out, "Phil Proctor. Why are you here? Are you back here for good?"

"I've come back to you, girlie, haven't I," he replied, his hands still resting on her hips, his breath blowing hot on her right cheek. He then curled the long fingers of his right hand through her own and continued, "I don't know how long we have together, 'cos as you know, I am not a young man anymore. But I know we should give it a shot. You were on my brain, ma'am, the entire time I was away."

"That's okay with me. We should just enjoy every minute we have left."

That was all the words she wanted to hear from him. They leaned into each other and kissed again with a simmering intensity they would long remember. He then raised her up briefly, his hands spanning her waist and he gently slid her body down against his hardening crotch.

In the meantime, the local farmer mumbled something under his breath, got up from the café chair and walked out, heading home to cook his own meal.

****

Seven months later, a lot had changed in the small, but steadily growing, township of Brumby Flat.

Phil Duncan had the three-storey house, Bette's old home, finally up for sale on the real estate market. He was intent on staying in Adelaide with his new girlfriend Kimberley and their baby girl, Daisy Beatrix, who was named in honour of his late mother.

'The Raindrops Shop' had finally served its last customer a chai latte and closed its doors permanently. Raquel Willaston had left the Batty Roadhouse and returned to the local winery job she previously had.

Phil Proctor had immersed himself in one more silo project. He had told Raquel that he now had enough money to retire on. His modest apartment in New York overlooking Central Park was up for sale and there was a lot of interest in it.

On this particular lazy Sunday afternoon, with steady rain drumming against the iron roof and splashing against the windowpanes, Raquel tightened her bathrobe and fell back into her leather couch, clutching the latest bathroom design magazine in her hands. Near her bare feet, the fireplace glowed vibrant hues of red, orange and blue as flames licked around the fresh wood logs she had just tossed in.

Their blue heeler Maxine had chosen her position wisely by the fire, and was lying there, her eyes contently shut. Every now and again, her body and legs would twitch as she slept.

Proctor had moved into her house since he had returned. All the boxes piled high in her home had been finally dealt with. She was trying to work out the designs for the new house and land package they had bought together in the new Brumby Hills Estate. They were very lucky to get it, as the blocks in the new development had sold out lightning fast.

Phil Proctor walked tall into the loungeroom, also wearing his terry-towelling bathrobe and padding around in his bare feet. He smiled slightly and bent over her. She raised her face to him, and they kissed briefly. They had just enjoyed a warm shower together with Proctor giving her a slow fuck from behind.

"That was really nice," she said, as their lips and bodies parted. The open fire crackled away in the background.

"What are you doing? What you got there, girlie?"

"I wanted to look at some new bathroom designs. We bought a block together, to build our house. It's all so exciting."

Proctor pressed in again, his mouth hungry for more.

"But you're much more exciting," he whispered in her ear.

He parted her soft lips, his probing tongue flicked inside her mouth, and she felt herself getting hot and her pussy wet all over again. The bathroom design magazine slipped through her fingers and dropped onto the floor. Her thighs parted slightly as he knelt before her. They both started to breath deeper, as he shrugged the bathrobe off his shoulders.

"Want to come back to the bedroom, girlie? No work today, can't paint silos in this weather?" He asked, as his bright blue eyes glazed over. She leaned forward, kissing him firmly back as a sign of her consent.

Suddenly, the wall phone rang.

Raquel fell back on the couch and shook her head. "Ah. I can't believe you got the phone connected. Who connects an actual phone line these days? You're like some stone-age dinosaur."

He smiled at her smirking comment and sprang instantly to his feet. "Hold on, girlie. I'm not a dinosaur in the bedroom, alright? Howdy," he picked up the receiver and answered the call brightly.

There was a moment's silence. He listened intently before he put down the phone again wordlessly.

"Did I mention that I'm having lunch with my friend Geena tomorrow?"

She turned to look at him when there was no response from him. She could not read his facial expression, other than she noted that he looked strangely puzzled.

"Phil, who was it? Are you okay?"

"Well. That was our builder Andy on the line. He said you may want to see this. He said we have to come up to see our block right now."

"Oh, okay. Why is that?"

He took a deep breath and swept his damp grey hair back, away from his vibrant blue eyes. "I can't believe it. They've uncovered a body, he said, buried on our land. Said they were about to start on the foundations. Then I hung up. I didn't know what to say…to that kind of news. Never expected to hear that…"

His voice trailed off and his last words hung in the air. There was an uncertain silence, except for the roar and sizzle of the open fireplace.

She finally looked up at him, biting down hard on her bottom lip. "Well, that certainly changes a lot of things."

"Yep. Sure does, girlie. It seems we've bought ourselves the wrong block to build our dreams on."

She studied his blue eyes intensely, raised an eyebrow and said simply, "Oh shit."

To be continued in 'Dead Goes The Neighbourhood'